CW00546861

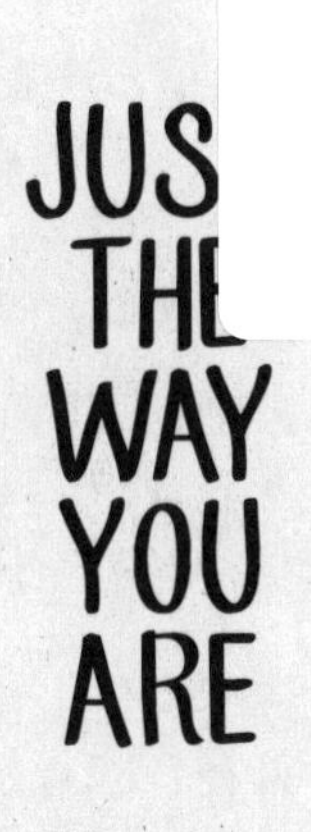
WAY
YOU
ARE

JUST THE WAY YOU ARE

SANJEEV RANJAN

RANDOM HOUSE INDIA

Published by Random House India in 2014
1

Random House Publishers India Pvt Ltd
7th Floor, Infinity Tower C, DLF Cyber City
Gurgaon – 122002
Haryana

Random House Group Limited
20 Vauxhall Bridge Road
London SW1V 2SA
United Kingdom

978 81 8400 634 6

Typeset in Bembo by R. Ajith Kumar

Printed and bound in India by Replika Press Private Limited

A PENGUIN RANDOM HOUSE COMPANY

To my mom who has always loved me
but whom I always misunderstood

The one thing we can never get enough is love.
And the one thing we never give enough of is love.

—Henry Miller

PROLOGUE

Indira Gandhi International Airport, New Delhi

IT WAS STILL QUITE EARLY in the morning when I left home for the airport. Spring in Delhi is a blessing: flowers in dazzling colours and lush green leaves greet you wherever you look. Now it was receding and giving way to summer, but the remnants of flowers were scattered on the ground, giving all a joyful outlook. It was slightly nippy for 7.30 am but the weather in Delhi is as erratic as a woman's moods these days. I smiled at the thought of women and looked out the window to divert my mind. There were only a few cars and buses moving towards their destinations on the empty roads. Instinctively, I lowered the window of the cab and felt the breeze ruffle my hair. The mild sunshine kissed me, and I smiled widely.

I was as bright as the spring season today. I was excited about going to Switzerland, any young, romantic man's dream destination. It was also my first trip abroad. Well, I was also smiling at my fate, my destiny. My desires were usually fulfilled, and it seemed to me that the whole universe conspired to fulfil them. But never on time. There was, somehow, a delay—every single time. And probably the habit of getting everything in life after a lot of effort and waiting had made me patient.

I turned to the driver's eyes in the rear-view mirror and asked him how much more time it would take to reach the airport.

He also looked up at the mirror and perhaps at my eyes in it. 'Sir, just about twenty more minutes if we don't get any traffic.'

'Traffic? At this hour!' I exclaimed.

'Generally there is no traffic at this hour, but who knows what one's destiny has in store,' he philosophized.

His spoke in a heavy Punjabi accent, and like a true-blue Punjabi, he had answered a straight question philosophically. Anyhow, who would know the depth of his words more than me, who had been betrayed by destiny more often than not. If destiny were a woman, she would be living with some great vengeance against me. A friend who had once read the tarot cards for me had sealed my fate years back: 'This Destiny woman would take time to befriend you, leave aside loving and pampering you. At least six years.' I had nervously laughed it off back then, but experience had taught me this better than tarot. I don't give up easily, so I was sure I would woo destiny someday in my favour.

The driver must have interpreted my silence as worry, and quickly pitched in, 'Arre sir, why are you getting so serious? I will ensure we reach on time.'

I merely nodded, discouraging him from taking the conversation to some other level. I didn't want my smile vanishing thanks to a philosophizing Punjabi guy, right at the beginning of a very important day.

What could I do in the cab? I had played a few games on my smartphone, and the FM stations played really slow, depressing songs in the morning. So I didn't have a choice but to look out at the city. Myriads of thoughts fought to make themselves heard in my mind, but I chose the easy way. I dug out my earphones and turned on the music in my iPod that my brother had gifted me a few years ago with his first salary.

The driver gave me an 'I-told-you-so' smile when he parked in front of the airport entrance twenty-five minutes later. I paid him the decided amount and he drove off after handing my trolley bag to me. This was the first time I was going to *enter* the airport. I had been here only once before, and that only to see off my girlfriend, Shagun.

As I dismissed thoughts of Shagun and started walking towards the entry gate, my mind went blank and I felt like a little kid who had been left at a new place, all alone, not knowing what to do. I called up my brother, who is an avid traveller. The telephone ring went unnoticed, just the way I had not been noticed by many till now. Fair enough, everything must have been messed up at home and the chances of their answering the phone would be slim. So I dialled Rakesh's number, who is one of my very close friends, but I guess it was too early for anyone to be up and taking calls. Finally, I called Gaurav, my Facebook friend with whom I had come to share a very good relationship over the years. Luckily, he answered the phone.

'Hello, young man. Congratulations!' he exclaimed in his usual peppy yet relaxed tone.

'Thanks so much, yaar, but I am angry that you didn't turn up,' I said jovially.

'Come on, man! I am so sorry for that. My mother suddenly developed some acute pain in her knees and I had to rush back to my hometown and take her to the doctor. Anyway, this is a quick trip. I landed in Bhopal two days back and am flying back to Delhi tomorrow. Then we can sit together for a party again, why worry!'

'I get all that, but the party is postponed for now.'

'Why, you stingy guy? I won't leave you till you give me a party,' he said determinedly, laughing at the same time.

That made me laugh too. 'Arre, who are you calling stingy! I am going to Switzerland, and that too in the next couple of hours. I am at IGI airport.'

'What, Switzerland? Couple of hours? How? Why?' He said it all in one breath, and I couldn't help but laugh.

'Credit Suisse has offered me a job. They called me this

morning itself, and even sent me the tickets. I was given an option of taking up the job and flying to Switzerland on urgent basis, or ...'

'Or what? And why today? You got married last night, you fool! And today you are going to Switzerland! Alone! Completely preposterous! I am sure your wife would never take you back in, man. If I were your wife, I wouldn't have!' he said glumly, more astonished than happy.

I was sad to think that I was going alone, but gathered myself quickly and said, 'Didn't you see that coming in your tarot cards, pal? Didn't you tell me my fate is a woman out to kill!' I snickered, and heard him laugh too.

'That's true, man,' he said while snorting. 'You and women! Either you don't get one, or can't stay with one. Stay away from me, lest you pass on your luck with women on to me too.'

'Chuck all that about women, and help me with something. I called you to ask how to proceed further from the entry gate of the airport.' He chuckled and I quickly added, 'Yaar, come on! I am travelling by air for the first time and need your help. Tell me!'

Eventually, he detailed the process for me (not before teasing me no end about being away from my new wife and the way I had gotten scared of the airport itself). We disconnected with warm pleasantries, wishes for his mother's good health, and his promise to make it to my reception, whenever and wherever it happened.

On a parting note, he said, 'Don't worry, pal! Things will be fine. I know how difficult it is to choose between two things you have longed for, for years.' I had nothing to say to him; he was one of the few who understood. And then he smirked, 'Have loads of Swiss chocolate and women, mate!'

'Oh yes, that is why I am not taking my wife with me, because I would love Swiss chocolate more,' I shot back.

I moved in through the main gate and was greeted by a thick, white moustache; there was a tiny, dark face hiding behind it. The security guard's moustache reminded me of those south Indian actors who can scare you by merely smiling at you. I suppressed a smile and moved in after showing him my tickets and driving license as identity proof. The queue for putting the luggage through the scanning machine was as long as an anaconda. I wondered where all these people were going. I joined in, but was soon lost in thought.

Yesterday was my wedding day. I am thirty-two. I got married after much ado. Today, I am travelling to Switzerland. Alone. Brilliant!

I

1

MY BAG WAS SAFELY INSIDE the scanner and I was at the mercy of the guard who was frisking men shamelessly. As he ran his hands along the length of my body, I felt strange sensations. I didn't understand why these people could not use machines to scan people too. The moment I stepped down from the wooden platform after the too-close-for-comfort frisking, I heard the man behind me shouting, 'Hey, keep your hands off me!'

'Please cooperate, sir, there is a terrorist threat at the Delhi airport today and we cannot take any risks.' The security guard had a strong, dominating voice.

The man gave in, but the information scared me. I really did not want to look at everyone around me suspiciously, but then who knew who could be a terrorist.

As I stepped further ahead, there was a series of trolleys loaded with bags and suitcases all around me. I was annoyed at the luggage traffic, to say the least, because people kept bumping them into somebody or the other's foot.

'Oh god! Why the hell are they carrying their entire home packed in a suitcase with them? Are they smugglers?' I complained to myself. But the idea sounded pretty weird to me, so I rejected it outright. I am sure Indians have a tendency to pack a lot of food in when they travel. Some vegetarians feel that vegetarian food abroad will not be sacred enough for their consumption, so they carry a suitcase-ful of eatables for 'emergency use'. It felt no different from a railway station at this corner, where people were ready to run their luggage wheels over anyone's foot to take a place in the queue for the boarding passes.

In the meantime, my black bag slid out of the scanner on the conveyer belt and I grabbed it with both hands. It was only when I noticed a couple of people staring at me that I realized that nobody else would have taken it anyway. I made a mental note that I was travelling abroad now and should be calm, lest some security guard with monstrous moustaches get suspicious. I turned my bag over on to its wheels and began rolling it towards the counter. But hold on! The drama didn't end there.

As for everything else, life had a different plan for the momentous occasion of my first time travelling by air; it was to be memorable for me in more ways than one. Amidst the shoving and shuffling, I made my way to the end of the queue. That's when I heard someone say, 'Excuse me!'

I didn't want to turn back; it could have been someone

calling someone else. Or had the security guard with the huge moustache found my observing people suspicious? I cursed under my breath, 'Why the hell did I have to stare at people's luggage!' I pretended that the 'excuse me' was not meant for me and kept moving. Just then, as if out of thin air, a young lady in her mid-twenties landed right in front of me. I was bewildered and almost shrieked. But as I swallowed my surprise, I also jumped back one step.

'Excuse me? What's wrong with you?' I exclaimed.

'I am so sorry about this,' she stammered, probably embarrassed at my reaction. She pointed at my feet and I looked down immediately, wondering what I had wrongfully stepped on.

She smiled and said, 'The trolley bag. It's mine.'

I automatically clutched the handle of the bag handle tighter—was she a thief? At an airport! She looked well-dressed. But I still waited for her to speak.

'I guess we have the same black bag. You pounced on my bag so violently and dragged it off the conveyer belt, that I couldn't stop you in time.'

When I looked at the bag in her hands, I realized it looked almost the same as mine. Okay, it was mine; I noticed the name tag flashing my initials in bold black letters. The confusion was now clear and I felt sheepish at having grabbed the bag with such gusto. I apologized quickly, not wishing to look like a bigger fool, and exchanged her bag for mine.

I quickly went to the counter and waited for my turn, still feeling embarrassed about the bag episode. My ears turned red wondering if the woman was standing somewhere behind me and if she thought I was dumb. But when my turn came, I forgot all that and picked up my stamped boarding pass.

I walked into the plush waiting lounge that looked nothing less than a grand hall, beautifully designed, with several pieces of art as well as restaurants lining the sides. There was still over an hour for boarding to begin. From what Gaurav had told me, a bus would come and drop off the passengers till the aircraft, and that it would be announced. So I did not bother too much about it and relaxed. It had been a long night, a very long night.

I took the corner seat of the waiting lounge on purpose, so that I would not be disturbed by anyone, even by mistake. In that corner, there would be no mistake with bags, words, or people. Plus, I had to call Mom; she must have become super-restless by now.

I dug out my phone from the deep pocket of my brand-new trousers. I wondered how I had acquired so many new clothes around the wedding time, and how all of them had been packed into my luggage, still folded and some still in clear plastic wrap. As I unlocked my phone, a message flashed in bright red: '10 Missed Calls'. As I pressed the screen at random places to reach 'Mom' in my phonebook, I knew I would get to hear some harsh words. I had not been able to speak with her before leaving home; everything was in a state of chaos when I left. All ten missed calls were from her number. I readied myself with a list of excuses for having missed her calls, and also for the second *Mahabharata*.

It had barely started ringing when I heard her sweet voice reach my ears at a screeching volume, piercing the quiet around me.

Without any hellos, she started off: 'Why did you not pick up the phone? I have called you so many times. One, you don't meet your mother and go, then you don't take her calls. Didn't you think taking my ashirwaad would make your journey better? You are going to phoren, it's not a small thing …'

'Mom … breathe!' There was silence for a moment, so I took the cue and rattled off my practised excuses, 'I was in the cab. You know I was in a hurry. We have been going crazy with the packing and everything, don't you know? I am not even sure if I have kept all the necessary things.'

The mother in her woke up, but the disappointment at not having seen me was clear in her voice. As also the mild anger in it. 'I don't know. You know well I have never touched your things, nor I ever will. Why should I get bothered by this?'

'Okay, Mom. Forget that, I will manage. I have reached the airport and the formalities are all done. I am waiting for the bus to pick me up. Okay?'

'What? Bus? But you told me you had to go by plane!' She sounded thunderstruck, my drama-queen mother.

'Oh Mom, the bus will pick me up from the airport and drop me till the plane. It's quite far away from the waiting room.' When I heard a 'Hmm' of understanding, I asked her, 'So what do I get for my dear Mom from Switzerland?'

'Swizzarland? Beta, where are you going? Your father was saying that you are going to phoren? I thought it is Amreeka.'

'Mom, it's Switzerland and it's in Europe. Trust me, it could be equally good or even better than America. Oh sorry, Amreeka.' I smiled at my innocent mother. She had managed to make her children good people, and successful at that. That was her wealth of a lifetime and she was blissfully unaware about things outside the home domain.

'You-rope! What's this now? I am not even able to say the name properly. Couldn't you have gone to some place with an easier name?'

'Mom, leave it na. For now, I am going to Europe. And I will bring chocolate for you; Swiss chocolate is famous all across the world.'

Hearing the word 'chocolate', her voice melted a bit, 'Chocolate! The ones that they show in these fancy ads on TV?' I assumed she meant dark chocolate and assured her I would get the best ones.

She seemed happy now, so I asked her, 'And anything for Dad?'

'Don't you know him? He never asks for anything. So get whatever you like for him; he will never say no to you.'

'Where is he anyway? I couldn't talk to him properly. He was quite angry over my decision in the morning. I tried soothing him down but he just rushed out of the room, looking worried and angry. I couldn't even tell him what going to this company means to me. Bhaiya told me ...'

'Don't talk about him. You know, last night at the wedding, he spilled dal on his brand-new suit *again*, right in the front. And with the dal all over the front of his suit, he was roaming around meeting people and dancing. I am really tired of this man. Explain something to him when you talk to him. He is seventy years old and does things like a child.' She had loved him for too long to not complain of the same things again and again. I knew she loved him for these little things only. She would have been disappointed if he had not spilled something on his clothes.

'Mom, did Dad dance?' I chuckled, trying to recall when that had happened.

'Oh yes! He was on Cloud Nine. And he ate as if he wouldn't ever get food after this. Now he has settled in the bathroom since morning. There are so many people around and all he can do is stay in the bathroom. I am sure as and when people wake up, they will break the door down to relieve themselves,' she sniggered.

I started laughing. This was the woman who had borne everything with a smile to give us a good life, and I was happy she was content now. While I was still imagining the bathroom door being banged by some relative, she hopped on to another topic.

'Beta, listen! Now that you are going to videsh, can you please get me a leather handbag, like the one that Shalini aunty has? She told me her brother bought that bag from Amreeka. But you are going ... where are you going? Oh haan, what should I tell the relatives?'

'It's Switzerland. And no need to boast about this to anyone.'

'Why not? They show off every time they buy anything. My beta is going to phoren and I should not show off? No way!'

'Mom ...'

'What? You never allow me to do anything.'

'Mom ... Okay, do what makes you happy. And don't worry, I will bring four handbags for you. By the way, who's Shalini aunty?'

'You know Shalini aunty, Sharma ji's wife. That fat lady?'

'No idea.'

'How can you not have an idea? You have even met her twice. Remember when she had made laddoos when her daughter got a job in Bangalore and she came over to make me feel jealous? And the other time when ...'

'Mom ... how does it matter?'

'Haan, that too!'

'I will bring handbags of my choice. And I know you

will like all of them.'

'But you are not going to Amreeka. Will you get it from wherever you are going?'

'Yes, my dear Mom. I will get them from Amreeka if you want them only from there. Don't worry! You take care of yourself and Dad. I will disconnect for now; the announcement will be made any moment.'

'Listen, listen! You asked for everyone. What about Shagun?'

'Oh, what does she want?'

'Huh, she is your wife. You should know about it more than me. And someone was mentioning this morning that she was your girlfriend before you got married. Then I am sure you know it better than me ...'

'Okay, I will see on my own. Is she sleeping? She was awake when I left, I had asked her to take rest.'

'Yes yes, I also asked her to sleep. Nobody will disturb her till she wants to get up, don't worry! But tell me, was she really your girlfriend before marriage? You never told us.' Then, as if she had remembered something suddenly, she said, 'Now I know who you spoke to all night over the phone!'

'Mom,' I said, ignoring her, 'I am being called, I am going. Bye for now. And one more thing, my phone will be switched off for long; it's a very long flight and I will call you tomorrow after reaching Bern.'

'What burnt? Didn't you just tell me you are going to

Swizzarland? Then You-rope? You confuse me!'

I was too tired to explain, so I quickly said, 'Mom, it's Switzerland's capital. I will tell you later. Bye now.'

Before she could say another word, I hung up. Soon after, I heard the announcement, hopped into the bus, and, within the next ten minutes, was on my first-ever flight.

Switzerland, here I come!

2

MANY WOULD SAY I WAS lucky to have a job to my liking, a newly wedded wife, a settled family, and all the basic needs and many comforts that one could hope for. I wonder if people realized that it never came together; something had to be sacrificed for something else. As I took my comfortable window seat in the dimly lit flight, my mind wandered to the rushed events of the past few days. I patted my back on having successfully accomplished a task of humongous proportions.

Just then, I heard a commotion in the aisle just ahead of my seat. I stretched my neck to see the cause, and there it was—a petite woman hiding her face behind her boarding pass, perhaps trying to search for her seat number by scanning the small lettering on the pass from up close. Pretty close, actually. Since she had all her attention on the pass, she had bumped into another passenger who had been trying to put some luggage into the overhead cabin. I was wondering at her clumsiness when she stopped right where I sat and settled in the empty seat next to me. Lo, it was the same woman whose bag I had taken by mistake. She had recognized me too. We shared a customary stiff smile. I was not in the mood for conversation, nor was I lucky when it came to women anyway. So I just looked out the window at the ground staff running around. It didn't take too long for me to slip into my thoughts, despite the fidgety woman seated next to me.

The last few days had passed as if in a daze; so much had happened in between that thinking back felt like replaying the reel of some Bollywood love story. Till a few hours back, I had felt like the luckiest and happiest man on earth. All my dreams had come to life, one after the other. I could see a blissful future ahead of me, that too with the girl of my dreams, someone I deeply loved.

I had waited for this night for very long, and so had my ever-so-loving mother, who was the only one to not have given up on dreaming about my marriage. All others had had their doubts in some form or the other, given my age and particular expectations from my partner. When the rituals began, I was excited; when they had been going on for a few hours, I started getting tired; after a few hours, I was praying for it all to end soon; and when it finally ended, I was dead tired. Who wouldn't be! The running around for the day had started pretty early and the ceremonies had ended at 4 am the next day. I couldn't figure out how the excitement of getting married was supposed to keep me running in the face of a long day and night to come, hordes of relatives to be managed, and the emotional setting at the girl's side at the end of it all!

I wondered why putting sindoor in the bride's hair parting was the last ritual, albeit the most important after which two people are pronounced man and wife. Brian Tracy would have jumped into the very fire that I had to perform pheras around, or just strangled himself with the jaimala right there. He had died writing about prioritizing tasks; not really died, but you know what I mean! And here were these rituals, putting the most important at the very end. Wow! But whatever it was, I was exhausted and, in fact, felt I would pass out in the wedding mandap itself. I am an early sleeper and when the clock struck midnight, I was ready to call it a day. But my goddamn relatives had gone all wild and whiskyed, and were trying to make me dance and meet their godforsaken friends who I had no idea about, all through the night. I literally smiled my way through the people I met with subconscious ignorance, knowing well I wouldn't see more than half of them ever again.

I had decided on having a simple wedding after I watched *Hum Aapke Hain Kaun*. Only a few close friends and family members. But when I had presented this idea to my parents, my mother had feigned fainting and my father's eyes went so wide that I thought they would pop out. Their protests had even made me tell them that I was impotent and couldn't marry anyone. That was the last nail in the coffin. But my mother got up after that and tore into my idea—left, right and centre.

'What? Only a few relatives? Why?'

'Mom ...'

'Shut up! You know, you are finally getting married now, at the age of thirty-two; plus whose marriage will we have in the house after this one now? Your children or your brother's—nothing before that. We have so many dreams, so many wishes. We will do this function, wear this sari, and tease that Sharma's wife and all. We all have a birthright to celebrate and organize your marriage in a grand and lavish way. So don't give me faltu reasons to call off all the grand functions.'

'But Mom, I don't like all this. It's such a waste of money, all this stupidity.'

'You mean the whole world is stupid! You are calling us stupid?' She turned to my father, 'Hain ji, see what your son is saying!'

'Mom, what's with wasting money like that?'

'Wah! People across the country are stupid. It is only our son who is so intelligent. This is the day for which I have brought you up! To be denied these small happy moments, of flaunting my bahu and beta to the world. What has life come to!' She sighed deeply enough for me to get a warning signal that this conversation had started moving in a direction where I would very soon be left with no counterarguments to my mother's emotional state (read blackmail).

I understood that just like 'these young people of today' do not understand what elders say, 'these grown-up parents' will also not understand the logic of not wasting money on marriages.

So that day, after meeting all those people I had not been in favour of inviting in the first place, I was ready to drop. My home was in the same town but since my wife belonged to Agra, it was decided to arrange the wedding ceremony and all the related functions and rituals in Taj Mansingh Hotel. So guests from both the families had been accommodated there itself, and all arrangements had done accordingly. My father had made it clear that we would bid adieu to Shagun's family here itself and head home thereafter. I had assumed that many of our relatives were also leaving for their respective homes directly from there.

We had booked a couple of rooms in the same hotel. I thought I'd be able to relax, and Shagun too, before we finally left for home. It must have been equally crazy at her end as well. Shagun had been sent to a room with her family, and I to another. My close friend Sankalp was with me in my room and advised me to take some rest. I had just planned on taking my shoes off and reclining on the bed, when some distant relatives marched into my room to meet me. They were apparently leaving in an hour and wanted to spend some time with me.

'You have grown up from the last time I saw you.' I wondered when they had seen me, because I had not changed in appearance in the last seven- to eight-odd years.

I made the best out of the moment, 'Sorry uncle, I couldn't help it. I didn't have any choice except to grow up.'

'Very true! When I saw you the last time, you were so tiny.' One of the aunties, I don't know who, used her hands to show how tiny I was. From the size she indicated, I should have been a puppy more than a human. But she went on anyway, 'Now I am seeing you on your marriage occasion. Time passes so fast!'

To my chagrin, a lady standing at her side said without restraint, 'I am so happy for you. Finally you are married now. You mom was so worried for you.'

I nodded. I never understood why people asked or discussed such things. I could have asked if she let her husband touch her at this age, or if she was okay wearing short clothes. On the pretext, of course, that my mom was worried at her treating her husband like a dog. And imagine this: I didn't even know them properly. The only thing I could do for their most stupid and abrupt of questions was stretching my lips in a fake smile and nodding in a way that says, 'Thanks! Without your concern, I would *never* have been married.'

I was desperately waiting for the moment when they would leave the room and I could lie down for a while. I cared about my back, which was now screaming for a bit of rest, more than these uncaring, gossip-hungry relatives. I looked at Sankalp, anger dripping from my eyes. He smiled and winked at me to stay calm. After a minute, when they found me only nodding to every query, they decided to leave.

Sankalp knew I was about to bust a nerve; I was tired and these dialogues had managed to annoy me even more. So before I could say anything, he said, 'Yaar, why are you giving me the look? It's not my fault. I guess your dad instructed them to come here and see you. They just wanted to meet you and congratulate you.'

'Then they should have congratulated me and gone away. But did you notice, they did not say the word "congratulations" even once. I hate these meetings. I had told my mom very clearly to not invite anyone who I didn't know.'

Sankalp had nothing to say, so he preferred to remain silent. I thanked God that I could now take a nap for a couple of hours without any disturbance. But when has God ever let me be!

My mobile phone buzzed with an unknown number. I wanted to ignore it, but Sankalp drew my attention to it by mentioning that the number seemed from somewhere out of India. I looked at the screen closely but did not take the call; whoever it was could wait, I was sure. I relaxed and dozed off soon.

I woke up to the noise of feet rustling all around me; people were getting ready to leave. I woke up quickly, straightened my clothes, slipped on my shoes, and went downstairs. After that, it was a matter of a few more minutes. I stood motionless next to Shagun, not knowing what to do and how to react, as she howled, hugging her aunt and uncle. It was when everyone was crying in unison that my phone vibrated again. I dug it out of my pocket and saw the number flashing on the screen; the same number that I had seen a while earlier. Just as I was going to take the call, an old uncle, looking sad, turned and looked at me, perplexing me if nothing else. I didn't know what to do, as I was looking at my flashing screen and then at him, forcing a smile. He approached me with an almost pleading tone, 'Beta, please take care of our daughter. She is our only daughter and the apple of our eyes.'

I smiled at him, hoping he was done so that I could take the call. Two calls from an unknown foreign number had gotten me curious. He seemed ready with the next line but I gestured to him to give me five minutes as I was getting a call. I showed him my phone, and just as he adjusted his eyes to see what I was trying to show, I walked to one side where the howling was not that loud and took the call.

'Hello?'

'Hello, may I speak with Mr Sameer?' a firm, articulate

female voice greeted me from the other side. The accent was definitely not Indian; it did not seem American either.

'Yes, Sameer here. May I know who I am speaking with?' I said, pretty curious by now, and somewhat hopeful too.

'I am speaking from Credit Suisse, Switzerland.'

A thought crawled into my mind. Maybe it was a spam call saying that I have won a million dollars in a lucky draw in which I had never participated. I decided to hang up but then it happened. The woman with the strange English accent said something that brought a smile on my face. It was really a million-dollar call.

'I would like to inform you that this is regarding your application form that you had submitted on our website. We understand that you have abundant expertise in a field that we are looking to hire in. So, after due consideration, we would like to offer you a job with our organization.'

She had barely begun when I started mumbling, 'Thanks a lot.'

'There is just one catch to it. We have an urgent opening in that domain and you will be required to visit our Bern office for further discussion rightaway. What I I mean to say is that you need to start with us immediately and we will be arranging for the visa and tickets quickly if you accept ...'

My mind was going numb with each word she said, but I managed to gather my wits about me and tell her, 'But how is it possible? I got married a few hours back, lady. Isn't it possible to postpone this for a week or so?'

There was a pause at the other end and then she spoke again, this time commandingly, even calculatingly, 'Mr Sameer, we do understand your personal concerns, but I am sorry to inform you that it won't be possible to postpone it. We can definitely give you a week's leave once you come and join the office formally and understand your role and the office culture. In case you feel it is not going to be feasible for you, then you must let me know now, for I will have to fix up with the candidate second in rank of our preference for the same.'

I knew there would be ample time to curse my destiny after the phone call ended but for now, I needed to decide what I was going to do. 'What about the appointment letter?'

'Once you confirm, I will send the letter and tickets with all other details to your email ID in the next five-odd minutes.'

I managed a faint 'yes' before she rattled off again, 'Kindly take a printout of all the attachments, and carry the documents mentioned in the email. We apologize for this short notice but something critical has surfaced here. We really hope your journey is pleasant and also, congratulations on the job. And your marriage too! We are looking forward to receiving you here. If you face any confusion, please call me back on this number.'

I had barely said thanks when a beep indicated that the call had been disconnected. I was still for a few minutes.

Probably because I had been waiting for this call for three years, or visualizing the situation that was going to surface when I broke this news to all my relatives and, most of all, to Shagun.

What a wonderful time these people had chosen to call me, and what perfect timing! I got married a few hours back, and just when I was thanking my stars for the little bit of relief that I had earned, after the millions of questions and jokes relatives and friends had bombarded me with the entire previous day and night, this phone call had put me in a fix.

It was a tough call for me, no doubt, but I had decided. *Yes, I would go to Switzerland.*

3

'PASSENGERS ARE REQUESTED TO FASTEN their seatbelts and sit upright in their chairs. The aircraft will be taking off shortly.' The announcement broke my reverie and I noticed the girl next to me. She had already tightened the seatbelt around her waist, too tightly it seemed, but I didn't care much. I did the same, keeping enough space to enable smooth breathing, fiddled with the button to get my seat upright, but then saw that my chair was already aligned to the girl's. I assumed it was already straight and went back to staring out the window where people had now vanished and the craft seemed to be abuzz.

My parents had always wished to see me happy, and their current association of happy was always with marriage. Their dream to see me living with my bride had been postponed again. I was being tough on them, I knew. But it hadn't been easy for me either. True, I had taken the decision quickly enough to say this, but I also knew this was for me and Shagun. We had a lifetime of togetherness ahead, and my earning better would leave us with more to enjoy life with. Leaving my new wife, that too the very next day of the wedding, wrenched my heart. I had waited for this job and Shagun for the last three years. I was waiting for the day to make Shagun mine, make my better half a part of my life, inseparable against everything life put out. I had imagined her as my bride the moment I had seen her in the library, sitting alone on the corner seat. I was there to kill my boredom and satiate my hunger for knowledge. And she sat there in all her sweetness, oblivious of a boy staring at her with all his might. I hardly looked at girls otherwise; maybe I had accepted my fate of being a victim of unrequited love. In the same vein, I had left all hope on my parents, asking them to choose a suitable bride for me. But sadly the hunt had been unsuccessful, not because they had been unable to find anyone, but because I couldn't say yes to any of them. But this girl in the library had caught my attention.

The first thing that dazzled me was neither her blood-red salwar-kurta, nor her big, dark eyes outlined with kohl that she raised to look out the window, pondering over the book in her hands; neither her glossy red lips, nor her dazzling smile indicating that she understood the cleverness of the author and again immersed herself in the book. The book she was reading—*Midnight's Children* by Salman Rushdie—was the only book I had tried reading many a time and failed in the last few years. It could be the complexity of narration and storytelling, but there was something about this book that had always tempted me. I had challenged myself that I would finish reading the book someday; that day hadn't come yet.

'Welcome, ji welcome. Kaku has brought the bride home, come, come everyone!' Greetings had started at the entrance of my home even before we could step near the threshold.

A crowd gathered around the main door of the house. I figured that my mother and a few other relatives had left the hotel earlier than to prepare to welcome us, the newlyweds. My mom looked splendid in her Kanjeevaram sari, and more so with her trademark brilliant smile that was a sure sign of her happiness. She stood ahead of all other ladies like their leader. All others were also wearing their best saris and were coated with layers of make-up, this perhaps being the last ritual in the ceremonies that they could deck up for. Looking at their happy faces, I thought about my plan of breaking my news to them, and their smiles turned into gloomy frowns in my mind's eye. I still hadn't found a time suitable enough to break the news and I also knew that nobody was going to believe me right now, or even pay attention, in their ecstatic frame of mind.

There was a grand welcome and after the customary tilaks welcoming us, we were each asked to put our right foot forward and step in, only to walk into a roomful of aunties and some kids running around for no fathomable reason. My mom knew very well that I didn't like these rituals, but then I also knew that Mom would never listen to me, at least in this matter. So I gave in; I was too tired to protest and too excited about the new opportunity, which I still needed to announce.

All the aunties looked at me as if I had won a war and made them proud; I knew some of them closely enough to know that my marriage was going to be the topic of discussion for days to come. They were going to narrate my entire story, right from making a war strategy to such a grand reception, to anyone who was willing to hear them out. I gave them the smile that politicians give random people on meeting them, knowing that meeting again would be very unlikely. I tried to tell my mom to wrap up these rituals as soon as possible but every single time she looked back at me with a smile, taking her own sweet time doing things her own way. She was the happiest woman today and there would be no stopping her.

I had lost count in the last one night of the number of times I had to lower my head for the tilak to be put on my forehead. First it started with the leader, my mom, who did a little extra thing and stretched my cheeks like she did when I was a kid. And after that, the whole gang of aunties who were ready with their plate full of flowers and a diya, all came to me one after the other to put a tilak. One of them came close enough for me to notice her jewellery and stained teeth. After doing all the boring tika things, she murmured to me, 'Bahu is so beautiful. Finally your mom is happy, now that you are married.'

My forehead had begun to feel heavy under the weight of all the tilaks. It felt like an overload of jam on bread. To my relief, all the ladies soon turned towards the bride to complete some special customized rituals. I wished her all the best in my heart; it was her turn now.

I rushed towards my room. I had a lot of things to do before I could reveal my plan to my family: your son or brother or whatever I was to you was not going to celebrate his first night with his new wife, but was going to a far-off place for some urgent work. I had to read the call letter, take the printout of the ticket, and manage my luggage. For a moment, I was jealous of Shagun because all her bags were packed. If she had to go, she could just have rolled her bags out and that's all. Putting that thought away, I switched on my laptop and ran into the washroom to change into comfortable clothes. I logged into my email and downloaded the tickets and the call letter. I read it with unwavering, unfaltering concentration.

I had to pack up my stuff too. So I opened my almirah, dug out a trolley bag, and stuffed whatever I could think of into it. I did not want to shock everyone in the house, which was a hell of a lot of people to begin with. I made up my mind to speak to Dad first.

He was fidgeting with some people over payments,

bargaining like a typical middle-class gentleman. I broke the news as simply as I could, and then felt that everyone around me had gone quiet. I looked around—no Shagun, no aunties. Only some men and my brother. The women had apparently taken Shagun and settled her into my room, sorry, *our* room. It was deathly quiet when some women came out, laughing and teasing me about my new bride. When they saw everyone staring at each other uncomfortably, they also became subdued and asked about the cause. Everyone was aghast when I told them that I was going to Switzerland. Almost everyone was agape. I had expected this reaction, even a reaction worse than this, so I decided not to explain anything though my dad asked me several times and kept roaming behind me as I gathered stuff from around the dishevelled house. I moved into my parents' room to search for some important documents that I needed.

'Why are you going right now? Can you not wait for just a few days? What will I tell Shagun's people? You know this is not the right time.'

'Dad … I know, but the situation is such. I have waited for this for a very long time and you know it,' I said, looking for my passport. The entire house was in a mess, thanks to the marriage preparations, and I was having a tough time getting my things together.

'But why are you going? Couldn't it be a few months from now, so that Shagun could perhaps go with you?'

'Dad, it's my dream. And I can't let this opportunity go.'

'Do whatever you want to do!' He was angry, but I knew his concerns were legitimate. 'As usual, you never listen to me. Who am I!' he bellowed and left the room.

When I came out, everyone was looking at me and my father was nowhere to be seen. Ignoring everyone else, I moved towards my room. I knew this drama wasn't over yet. In fact, the real one was still to unfold.

I walked towards the room, strategizing what to say to Shagun and how. It was then that the whole bunch of relatives, except Mom, Dad, and my brother, rushed to stop me and said, 'Wait, wait! You can't enter this room as of now.'

'Can't enter? What do you mean? It's my room.'

'Yes, it's yours, but not for now. The rules say that you have to wait.'

I was really tired of these rules, and decided there and then that I would definitely read about them and find out who made them when I was back. But the need of the hour was to shoo away these relatives. I called on my mother to defend me, and soon after, she took charge and let me go in.

I finally entered the room, quickly turned around, and bolted the door. I looked at Shagun; she was sitting in the middle of the bed, her heavy red dupatta half covering her face. She looked gorgeous in the dimly lit room and I fell in love with her all over again. I had waited for this moment for so long, and now that I was here, in the moment, I was battling time and needed to break my strange news to her. The room was beautifully decorated with flowers, the curtains were drawn, and everything was perfect. Someone had sprayed some fruity, sensual fragrance and the room smelled exotic. It felt like I was in heaven, with my princess right in front of my eyes. Looking at this wonderfully decorated room and Shagun, for a split second it came to my mind to call the woman who had turned my life topsy-turvy since the morning, and postpone this job. But the next moment, when I realized that I couldn't take this risk, I discarded my own idea and approached my biwi.

Gathering all my courage, I said, 'Shagun ...' Apart from this, I couldn't say anything and waited for her to respond.

She said nothing, apparently playing the role of new bride with full gusto. I wished she could comprehend the state of my mind, and also not react unexpectedly when I revealed my plans. I said softly, 'Shagun, at least respond to my words. You know me well, it isn't an arranged marriage.'

These words seemed to ease her a bit; she relaxed and I heard some ornaments tinkle, arousing my love for her anew. She nodded slightly. She was only trying to behave like a newlywed; she had all the right to do this.

'I am going to Switzerland!' I was out with it, and she threw her ghunghat back herself, to look at me with her big, black, beautiful eyes. This trick always worked with women.

'Yes. Rightaway!'

'But why are you in such a hurry for our honeymoon? And what's with this sudden plan? What will our parents say?'

'Er, Shagun, it's not our honeymoon, baby.'

She looked confused, exhaustion and sleep writ large on her lovely face. 'Then what? Who is going to Switzerland?'

I looked into her eyes and said, 'I got a call from Credit Suisse this morning.'

That's all I had to say and her expression changed. She looked at her hands and shut her eyes tight, very tight. I didn't know what she was going to say and I really wished she would understand the need of the hour. I knew I was being selfish by expecting this from her. I was ready for everything that she would have to say to me.

'Rightaway? And what about me?' she said softly, fighting a surge of tears and swallowing the lump in her throat.

'Shagun, they have asked me to join immediately. I requested them for some time and told them I have just gotten married, but since something urgent has surfaced there, they asked me to travel immediately or lose the opportunity.' I was also getting very emotional, because Shagun and I had fought a lot of battles to reach this day in our lives.

Just then, like my guardian angel, she touched my cheek with her hand ever so slightly. 'This is your big day, Sameer. Why are you upset?'

'You know my bad luck, Shagun. I got this call at a moment when I was stuck between love and my dreams. What was I to do?' A lone tear was almost going to drop from her pretty eyes and I couldn't see that, not today. I was earning pretty decently here and had the woman of my dreams. I thought I would refuse the offer and stay with her. 'I will not go if you are unhappy about it, Shagun, I promise!'

'Do you think I don't know you enough? I know you are foolish enough to stay back if I say so,' she chuckled amidst her tears. She looked even lovelier, her cheeks glistening with the tears she was trying so hard to stop.

'They have said that they will give me leave after joining and I also remember that we decided to have our honeymoon in the best place of the world. We will go for Switzerland once I complete all the formalities.'

She didn't say anything and to my surprise she stood up, walked around the bed, and came and stood very near me. Before I could say anything to her, to my surprise she planted her soft lips on mine and passed on her warmth to me. And with it the assurance that she had faith in me. She hugged me and whispered, 'I am sure you will devise a way to compensate for our lost first night.'

She smiled, and I thanked God silently for bringing her into my life. How lucky I was to have her! Patience indeed bears sweet fruit, I thought. I held her close to me and gave my erstwhile girlfriend-turned-wife a deep, passionate token of my love.

I had a lot to do, so she offered to quickly change and help me pack. She enquired as to where I kept my clothes and I directed her to the wardrobe. She went into the room to change into comfortable clothes. I went about collecting important papers and putting them into a file.

Little did I know that Shagun would find all my clothes in the right place and with it the diary that I had guarded with my life up till now. The diary that I had never showed her, even after she had asked so many times what exactly I wrote in it.

I was travelling to Switzerland; Shagun was ready to travel into the recesses of my mind through that diary. Our journey together had just begun. She had plunged into the tepid waters of my past in the diary while I had taken wings to an alien land. Shagun flipped over to the first page.

4

AT THE TURN OF THE year I had barely felt that I was ultimately over with 'it'. And the 'it' here refers closely and most accurately to my stupidity. But I didn't assume that that looking into the mirror, I would be so proud of myself. That was the first time I felt a tinge of regret inside me, taking shape, of what I was once. When I look back it is almost inconceivable to think of myself as an ambitious, no-nonsense, work-driven, ah, well ... with the liberty of adding a few more adjectives ... person. It was during those years that I used to run behind things that I thought unattainable when in reality they weren't even worth attaining or running behind. Age makes a person mature is something I never agreed to. I mean, maturity is something I thought I had inherited right from the day I was born. So, when people said that I needed to grow up I was nothing but indifferent to them. I was, in a way, sacrosanct. But majorly stupid. It makes me laugh out loud at the kind of things I did and worse, cried over them. Good that those things didn't happen ultimately, otherwise I would have been in a rut and not flying off to Switzerland at the moment. As I soar into the clouds with butterflies in my stomach I giggle to myself. I remember the 'good old days', though they weren't that good.

November 2011

Finally, I was to be in Delhi.

In my appointment letter 'Delhi' flashed in bold. I could almost do the bhangra at the mere thought of it. When I read the word, I spun two rounds and hunched over the dining table to read it again, fell on my back on the bed, and read it all over again. I may as well have been branded as a lunatic but for now only I knew what kind of importance Delhi held for me. I had been yearning to be posted in the city. I had heard a lot about it—its cafes, promenades, clubs, and girls, and, of course, its perfect couples. I could be one of them too—who knew where my better half was. Rakesh, my college buddy, had called me up, fidgeting over the postings. Apparently, everyone, for some weird reason, was being posted to Chennai, Kerala, and other places down south. I'm not a racist, I swear. But honestly, I have had enough. I couldn't have survived longer in that area. Be it language or people, I believe everything is good in its own way. But I don't find myself belonging to that part of the world. It's as simple as that. Rakesh, unfortunately, couldn't fight against his luck. I was very worried. Mom had asked me to accompany her to the market to buy some kheera and I stood there for a few moments in contemplation while a bull chewed its way to glory on the bunch of kheeras I was holding. Mom, as usual, had rebuked me, 'Tera kuch nahi ho sakta! It's a waste to bring you here.' I had been accustomed to her reprimands since childhood. I didn't even bother to listen. It flew right atop my head, slipping past my ears. What bothered me at that moment was the email from the recruiters. Rakesh's words kept hitting against my skull and my heart stalled on the way back home. What if I didn't get Delhi? What if I was left to rot in the heat of Kerala or for that matter Thiruvananthapuram? What if I ended up my whole life slicing coconuts and sitting by a kiosk for coconut water every evening after coming back from office? What if a certain lungiwala came with his daughter and abducted me and forced me to marry her? What if ... what if ... My head was fit to burst in no time. I rushed to my room, flipped open my laptop, and fought against the anxiety running through my nerves while the mail loaded. Ultimately I saw it. Delhi. And the rest is, of course, history. Saddi Dilli, here I come!

The train screeched and finally came to a halt at Hazrat Nizamuddin Railway Station. No train journey in India is fruitful until and unless it is late by a couple of hours. This is almost inevitable to mark as a subsidiary tribute to the legacy of Indian Railways, where time runs in a different dimension altogether. Here, though, it was four hours. This time, however, the heavens saved me. Though it ran late, I at least got my meals delivered sitting in the compartment itself. Otherwise it's such a headache to crane your neck like a vulture and scan restaurants at each station. And the food, mashaallah! I must say, Delhi showed itself to be promising right in the beginning. All along the journey, thoughts like invisible flies kept jutting in and out of my head—baseless, meaningless thoughts which under no circumstances could affect my life in the remotest of ways. Germany is going to attack Austria again. The turmoil in Egypt must end. Nigeria is still fighting for its civil rights, what a tyranny. What a waste too! At least I'm not one of those dumb, stupid assholes who keep dreaming of either Katrina or Kareena, or for that matter Vidya Balan. Why do people even watch Bollywood films? Well, there was a lot of junk inside my head. I hoped I didn't have OCD. 'Arre bhaiya, could you get me another cup of chai, please?' I asked the service boy. A group of teenagers was sitting by me, one virtually on top of the other. What will happen of this country, I wondered. I was lucky; I got the lower berth and skipped the hassle of going up and down every now and then to use the toilet, brush my teeth, or drink tea. I could easily wear my chappals and go for a stroll whenever I liked and use the toilet too. My luggage could be easily kept under surveillance, below the berth. And for now, I could slip the curtain back and let the wind play on my face as I thought of Delhi and the dreams to come.

After some time my eyes seemed heavy. I thought of taking a nap. Just as I closed my eyes for a couple of minutes, I found the service boy standing beside me. 'Sir, kuch chahiye? You want something? I could hardly open my eyes, though his words were clear in my ears. In my slumber, I mumbled to him to come back after fifteen minutes. I would be awake by then. He said that he could only come back after serving the entire compartment. I didn't bother to reply.

But to my surprise, he returned in five minutes. At least it felt like five minutes. And asked me again if I needed something.

I looked at him with a mix of surprise and admiration, and said, 'Whoa! Never did I expect such prompt service in the Indian Railways. Well, that was pretty fast, ha! I'm sure the Indian Railways can surely put forward its name to be included in the Seven Wonders of the World!'

He gave a hearty laugh at that. His upper pair of incisors came sticking out like a rat. After a few seconds, he composed himself. 'Sir, like you, almost all the people in the compartment are sleeping for the time being. They have asked me to come after ten minutes. So that's the case.'

I smiled at his words and didn't say anything. I pulled back the blanket and drew the curtains aside. The wind was on my face again. I leaned back and put the pillow behind me. It seemed to be tablecloths sewn together rather than a pillow; it was undoubtedly the world's thinnest pillow and hurt my back. So I slid my backpack behind me and rested my spine on it. That felt better.

All this while, the boy still waited and kept on requesting that I have my breakfast. He had the plate in his hand and held it close to my face. It was almost like a feat he had to perform—handing me the plate at this moment. He wore a pleading look. I smiled and took the plate from his hands. He gave me an ear-to-ear smile that surely must be an exact replica of what Ronaldo gives once he hits his final goal. I chuckled, watching him move ahead, sliding his basket on the train floor, asking the crowd if anyone else needed breakfast. I was about to unwrap my plate when it struck me. I called him back, 'Oye, listen.'

He rushed back, his sandals slapping on the floor, and asked, 'Yes, sir. Anything you want? Sugar or milk powder?'

'No. Tell me something—are you going to serve lunch as well?' I asked, sipping the tea. It tasted insipid.

'Sir, we aren't very sure about it. If the train reaches Delhi on time then we won't serve but if it gets delayed by two or three hours, then we will probably serve it. We'll surely let you know by 11 am. By the way, can you tell me what is the time right now, sir?'

In a reflex movement, I looked down at my wrist. And there was no watch. I hadn't worn a watch for the past six years. So I quickly took out my phone and pressed it on. 'It's 8 am.'

He nodded and said again that he would let me know about lunch by 11 am. I had my breakfast and looked outside. There was nothing else to do. The train had become unexpectedly slow. I could count the trees in the fields passing by. I was having about doubts about the train making it on time as it was moving at snail speed. They claim it is the fastest train of India. Well, if they say so!

Around 11.30 am, the serving boy came to my berth and said, 'Sir, the train has got delayed by three hours and it can be expected to reach Delhi by 3 pm.'

'Expected,' I sighed and mumbled, 'True.' Nothing can ever be said absolutely about train journeys in India, at least until the train actually reaches the destination. Till then everything is murky. It might even get delayed by thirteen hours, who knows.

I thanked him. Other people were enquiring about the train timing as well. I saw him moving ahead to clarify their queries. Some of them were quite annoyed about the delay. Naturally! And then of course the criticism of the ministry was about to begin. People started cribbing about the downfall of the present government and what one should and should not do after becoming the railway minister. One of them had to catch another train from Anand Vihar and he was fuming, furiously spilling acid and slang on the system. I had a strange urge to laugh but it was fear, in truth, that held me back. 'PILs. Damn PILs should be filed against the government, I tell you. Bloody morons,' I heard him shrieking. It reminded me of a similar incident I had experienced around four years back. The train I was in had got delayed and I couldn't reach on time to take my engineering entrance exam. Since then I have had this inordinate obsession to get out of this country as soon as possible. Hopefully I will be lucky someday.

After getting to know that the train would be delayed, all the passengers drew back their curtains. I also drew back my curtain and wondered what was next in store for me.

I didn't know anyone in the city and it was also not clearly mentioned in the appointment letter to which centre they might post me. It could either be Noida or Gurgaon. I had always under the impression that the office might be somewhere in central Delhi. But one of my friends surprised me when I told him that the company had posted me to Delhi.

'Delhi? As far as I know there is no office in Delhi except the administrative office, and that too in PTI building,' he said. 'It will be in either Noida or Gurgaon.'

'Er ...' I silently panicked, thinking what to do now. And the very next day, I got an email to report to the Gurgaon office but it wasn't mentioned anywhere which office I was going to get and it really confused me.

My dad, at the time of leaving me at the station, asked me where I was going to stay for the first couple of days as he was a bit worried as we didn't any relatives in Delhi with whom I could have stayed. I had fortunately already spoken with Satyan, one of my school friends. He stayed in Greater Noida and had asked me to stay at his place for as many days I liked. Dad relaxed on learning of this. He knew Satyan well and hence was relieved.

'Did you talk to him?'

'Yes. I spoke with him yesterday itself. He asked me not to worry about PG accommodation and other stuff. He reassured me that it is easily available. The only thing that I need to worry about is the location of the office. So initially, for the first couple of days, I might stay at his place,' I said.

Dad still didn't find my words too reassuring. He seemed sceptical as he sank down on a chair on the platform and stared blankly ahead for a while. After some moments of silence, he came up with one of his weird solutions, 'If it's a matter of a couple of days, you can even stay in a hotel. You can find a good number of hotels near the station. I was there.'

'Okay. I will inform you when I find a suitable place to stay.' I touched his feet as the train came in.

It always made me smile, sheepishly though, whenever Dad talked about his trip to Delhi. That was some ten years back. I have a very vague recollection of it. But in my memory, Dad is still young and ignorant of how the world has changed in these little years. A decade doesn't actually feel like a decade when nothing around you changes, except for the paint on the walls or the tube-wells replaced by running pipes. As far as I could remember, it was the trade fair for which he had visited Delhi way back then. He had often said that back then Rs 100 notes looked more like today's Rs 1000 notes. The way a Rs 1000 note gets spent the moment one steps out of home, a Rs 100 note too had a similar lifetime then. Things were different. One could not have bought everything with money back then. At least not Dad's innocence.

I had nothing to do except sit around and hope that the train would pick up speed, so I called up Satyan. I had to let him know about the delay in my arrival. We would need to reschedule our meeting. I took out the phone from my pocket and dialled his number.

After few initial rings, he answered. 'Hello.'

'Hey, Sameer here,' I said excitedly.

When he repeatedly kept saying 'hello hello', it appeared to me that because of the noise and commotion in the train, he was unable to hear me clearly. But soon enough, he recognized my voice.

'Are you out?' I asked.

'Yes.'

'Okay. So what time are we meeting today? I just called to inform you that my train is late by three hours.'

'Yaar, I am sorry. I am actually going home for Diwali. It was so sudden that I couldn't even inform you. I am in Agra and will catch the train from here.'

'Oh.'

'And everyone else in our flat has left for home. And it's locked.'

'So when will you be coming back?' I asked, a bit nervous.

'Not sure about it. It all depends on the availability of tickets, you see. If possible, please make some other arrangement. Once I come back, I will search for a PG for you. It's not a big deal, trust me.'

I had nothing more to say. 'Okay, sure. Thanks.' I hung up and stubbed the phone on the seat. It toppled over like my hopes. Hope. Ah! That's surely the wrong word. Not to be found in my dictionary, at least, I thought bitterly.

I went completely blank after that. I didn't know what to do and whom to talk to. I could not believe that people could be so callous. He could have definitely called me once or maybe texted me. Was he lying? It's difficult to say nowadays what kind of notions people harbour in their minds. Or maybe Delhi makes you such. Dunno! Anyway, I had to figure out the next POA now. Dad was actually right. You never know where you may end up therefore a hotel seemed to be the ideal solution for the time being. I hoped the train would reach before it turned dark. It would otherwise be difficult to navigate through the city. Plus I had no idea which way to go look out for a good, cheap hotel.

I kept sitting by the window for a while, staring into

space, and then thought of calling up Gaurav. He had once told me that in case I found myself in any trouble in Delhi, I should let him know. He knew a good number of places. Affordable ones!

I called him. After three rings, he answered the phone.

'Hello, Gaurav. Sameer here.'

'Yeah, Sameer. Tell me. How are you?'

'Yeah. I am fine. I am about to reach Delhi in an hour or two but due to some problem, I may have to find myself a hotel for the time being.'

'Okay. No problem. Do one thing. Which station will you be reaching?' he asked.

'Hazrat Nizamuddin.'

'Okay. Take an auto from there to Paharganj. And ask anyone there about Hotel Priya Palace. They know me. You can give my reference also. It's quite affordable.'

I felt relaxed after this.

As expected, the train reached New Delhi at around 4 pm and with all my luggage, I somehow managed to reach Hotel Priya Palace.

I had come to Delhi for the first time. So I was naturally very excited. I picked up my phone and soon posted on Facebook: *Back to the relic root of India, with Khan's, parathe, Chandni, minars, and of course Sameer ... on a roll with Dilli!! Hellooooooo!'*

That week was very uncomfortable for me. First, I had to stay in the hotel and commuting was really difficult. And the HR head of my company was on leave. I had to wait till she got back and literally struggled to find the location of my office. This is exactly why I don't put much faith in companies in this country. They could have easily mailed me or it could have been a self-generating message where they could have let me know which office centre was to be assigned to me. Morons!

Then it was Diwali. It was the first time that I had to spend the festival alone in a hotel. I was sad and flashes of home lit with candles and diyas streamed in my head like a film. The sound of crackers filled my ears and I could once again smell the familiar gunpowder-burnt air on the night, as I did on Diwalis spent at home. How might they be spending the day this year? The faces of my parents floated up like smoke in front of me and I could see the reflection of a faraway lit lantern on the wall of my room. I had a strange urge to run out and walk down the street but I was too sad. I finally decided that the perfect solution to such situations was Facebook. I logged in and scrolled down to find a shock awaiting me.

Satyan and his girlfriend had posted pictures on Facebook in an album titled: 'Diwali in Noida'.

I couldn't understand why he had lied to me. He kept asking me on Facebook how everything was. Had I found a decent accommodation for myself? Was my office centre location given to me? And if there would be any further difficulty, he would certainly help me find a better place to stay when he returned. I didn't bother to reply. I had had enough of shallow people in my world already.

Time never passes fast in such moments and finally I decided, after a long battle with myself, to go outside and explore Delhi. The nearest place that I could go was Connaught Place.

I roamed around Connaught Place and found that it lit up like a new bride. As far as the eye could see, there were people hustling and bustling about and the shops were practically choking with humanity. In the darkness of night light seemed to dance everywhere, from the glittering bangles on girls' wrists to the shining salwar-suits of aunty-jis, to pillars and posts draped in colourful banners. I tried to ease my restless heart by looking at all of it and then decided to return to the hotel. I asked the hotel boy to get me dinner in my room and decided to stay back in the hotel the next day as well. There was a two-day break for Diwali and the office would be closed. I never thought that the first year I would land a job would bring with it my worst Diwali experience. Plus staying alone somehow chafed at my heart and I couldn't be at peace. It was indeed painful, but I guess I had no other way than to think of the good times in years gone by and smile to myself.

Five hours of sleep was not at all enough for me. I had too much stuff going on inside my head, with all the sadness of being alone and helpless, and thanks to the people outside the hotel bursting crackers till the wee hours of the morning to the shrill tunes of 'Sheela ki jawaani' and 'Munni badnaam hui', I couldn't get back to sleep. I tried stuffing cotton balls into my ears and pressed my pillow against my temple. But has anything ever worked against the tenacity of Dilliwallas? I finally gave up and got out of bed at 5.30 am, shaved, and showered. I looked at myself in the mirror and found myself looking worn out. I looked gloomy and pulling a pretentious smile too didn't bring about any change. I took the metro and reached office at 9 am. I had checked the way on Google Maps and had roughly calculated the time. It was my first day of reporting and I had expected that the HR head must have returned. But she was nowhere to be found. I tried conversing with a couple of other people but they seem to have no idea where they belonged and if at all they worked in the same office. There was a boy who sat just across from her cubicle. I tried asking him if he knew about the placements or if he knew when the HR head would be coming in. He seemed disinterested, as if I wasn't even there. He was trying to solve something with a paper and pencil and seemed to be cracking the code for an upcoming war. It was only after I had repeated the same question thrice that he raised his head and looked at me as if suddenly life had burst into this world. He looked at me questioningly. I repeated, 'Sir, I am here to meet Ms Vatsala. I am a new associate. Could you let me in on when and how I will be able to see her at the earliest?'

He didn't say anything. I wasn't sure whether he was paying attention to my words or was lost somewhere, perhaps stuck in his coding. I wasn't expecting this kind of attitude. I repeated my question again. He just nodded. I couldn't understand what his nod meant. Was it a yes or a no?

I waited for a few more minutes in the hope that he might come to his senses and respond properly. But hope often disappoints you. And when it comes to me, it always disappoints me. It was just the beginning for me, I believe.

Disappointed, I left the room. I didn't know where to go and whom to meet. I took out the appointment letter again and checked the location of the office. It was the same office. I looked for the name and designation of whom I was supposed to report to. It was the exact same.

I came out. On my way downstairs, I passed a lady and thought of asking her. She was a bit aged and her body language was that of a top-class management honcho. I asked her. 'Excuse me, Ma'am. Could you please tell me where I can meet Ms Vatsala?'

'Are you a new associate?' she asked. The question rekindled a new hope within me.

'Yes. I was told to report for work today.'

'Okay.' She gestured to me to follow her and led me to the same room where just a moment back I had found the biggest code cracker of the world. What a nutcase!

He looked around everywhere as if seeking an answer

out of air and then slowly opened his mouth, 'Actually, she hasn't come in to office yet.'

Without waiting for me to say anything, she asked the guy, 'Rajesh, do you know when Vatsala will be coming in?' The guy, who was pretending a few minutes back to be busy as hell, replied without the lapse of a second, 'Um, I haven't seen her, actually. Just check whether her bag is there at her desk.'

'No. Her belongings are not here.'

'That means she hasn't as yet come in.'

She looked at me and said, 'Um, what's your name?'

'Sameer.'

'Sameer, Vatsala is not yet in. You can wait for her in the waiting lounge. Give me your contact number and she will call you if she comes otherwise you just come here and check in an hour's time.'

'Okay.' I gave her my number and plonked myself down in the waiting room.

It was already full with guys and girls. All seemed to be new joinees. The company hired more and more employees every year. More than it could pay at times. That's precisely the reason why engineers are underpaid. And with such companies coming to college campuses for placements, I was sure the number of employees would definitely surpass the population of Jaunpur or Hisar, for that matter. All of them were quiet. Pin-drop silence. Everyone looked as if they were pissing in their pants. Just one odd man sat in the middle of the sofa in front of me and seemed to occupy the entire length of it. He spoke in a voice loud enough to put many Indian politicians to shame. I looked around to scan the faces and bodies. The girls, except for a couple, were certainly beautiful. One of the guys was muttering under his breath, 'Why is it that we always land up in the kind of batch where either the senior or the junior girls are beautiful and we are left with the ugly ones?" I pretended not to have heard this and suppressed a smile. After some time, the couple of so-called ugly girls also seemed beautiful to me. This was the fate of depravity! The boy was by now was busy discussing with another sitting near him how the company tricked ugly girls into a single batch so that they could hand them similar job titles and profiles and the beautiful girls were secured for the best positions. It was all about marketing and getting the best benefits.

I heard his friend reply disdainfully, 'What can be done? It's all written in fate.'

I was almost agape at such a remark and whispered to myself, 'What the hell! Aren't they beautiful? Am I blind or was it the south India effect?

The impact of my four-year stay in south India during my engineering was so profound that I fancied that every girl in this world was beautiful. You could find the spunk in every other girl you met but not in a south Indian. Who knows, one day I might start dating a Nigerian girl. The third girl sitting at the end of the sofa was a bombshell. Her lips were so thick and juicy. What did they want—Mallika Sherawat?

I ignored them and waited patiently for the call.

Someone came down the stairs and shouted, 'Whoever is here to meet Ms Vatsala can leave and come tomorrow.' A few heads flew up in shock along with mine.

'Why?' all of us shouted together.

'She is on leave.'

'That means that after making us wait for three hours, you realize that she is on leave.'

He ignored this and shouted again, 'Those who are waiting for Ms Vandana can wait for her in the canteen. She is coming in ten minutes.'

Almost all the girls walked towards the canteen. No one followed behind me as I ventured towards the exit.

There were no girls in my domain expertise! What the hell! Was this my destiny? I left the office building.

Nothing seemed to go right that day. I couldn't sleep properly, nor could I eat or take rest. Everything was chaotic inside my head and the HR issue was making me completely worked up. The only respite was the weather. Surprisingly it was cooler and the breeze seemed to be very unlike Delhi. I was hungry too, so got myself some patties. I could keep the leftovers in my room in case I felt like eating more later. I decided to go to Connaught Place again. It would look different during the day. I was clearer then. A circular block of art, I would say. The architecture was British, no doubt, but now all of those buildings were replaced by mega-shopping malls and stores. It was grandiose everywhere. People came in hordes to buy things, some of them just lingering, enjoying the place, some licking ice-cream sticks and talking of the weather, all sporting shades and brands. In the inner circular block was a garden with young couples flirting around the bushes. Evening had come down like silk and the place looked spectacular. I was thrilled.

'Oh god! Where the hell did I spend my youth? The real heaven is here,' I whispered to myself when I saw the golden Delhi girls moving around flamboyantly. Their tongues rolled around the 'R's and their accent could give Emma Watson a run for her money! I was bowled over by their exclamations. I tried imitating them. But each time I did, my tongue stuck midway and my throat failed me. I laughed at myself. My tone seemed so rough and broken. Someday I would, I must strive to achieve what had escaped me so far. And speaking fluent English was definitely on the list. I too would give others a run for their money. Some of the girls had taken the arms of their boyfriends and were walking around the inner circle. Something pinched at my heart. I felt deprived all over again.

What could you have expected from someone who had spent four years of his youth in some remote village doing an engineering course? I had almost forgotten that there was a world outside and in that world, there were, of course, beautiful girls. Life had so far been an abyss of unending monotony and tedium. I had almost come to believe that beautiful girls were to be found only in TV ads and in movies. Whenever some of the boys, like me, cursed their fate of having landed up in this ghetto of darkness, guys from the metro cities would encourage us. They would ask us to not to let go of hope and assure us that beautiful girls were for real and were not just limited to TV and soaps. One day I was online on Facebook trying to the best of my abilities to befriend a new chick. 'So, what are doing? Checking out hot girls?'

'Yes, of course. Though our college has hordes of such girls,' I sneered.

He laughed. 'Really? When I first came here, I thought I'd set myself up with any of the college girls and get some bang-bang, but now I honestly feel that I must propose to my Dilliwaali friend or she might too get out of my hands. The system is changing too fast there, yaar.'

'Is it so? I mean, how?'

'Ah! The point is, in Delhi you will find every girl attractive and if someone is not then she will do it artificially.'

'Artificially? What do mean?'

'She will spend half her day in the parlour and spend all her father's money on perming her hair, getting a new hairstyle, and indulge in numerous other things like facial and massages and what not. Everything that can and will make her look no less than a Paris fashion-week model. Get my point? Heavy eyeliner, mascara, Zara, Jimmy Choo, Chanel, and Gucci … the list never ends. We too should run away from this college and open up a Zara franchise, I tell you!'

He continued, 'So what happens is, you find almost everyone committed. Even the most phatichar guys will have the best of chicks. Even if someone breaks up, within in a week he will get another chick and ultimately get committed.'

'What the heck, man! Really? I mean, what about emotions and feelings?'

'Emotions? Dude, which world are you in? One week of commitment and then jump into bed. The more you use your brain, the more girls will slip out of your hands. Remember, all of them like dumb guys. So, keep your emotions and feelings in the gutter.'

I grimaced.

'And what is the point of feelings and all? One gone and the next is in. Just one criterion. She needs to be hotter than the previous one. Haven't you heard the saying?'

'Which saying? I have heard so many of Oscar Wilde's and Jane Austen's sayings on love and romance.'

'Oh no, not Oscar Wilde. Why do you try to act so intellectual all the time? These people had nothing to do in their life and couldn't have a single good affair and hence kept on cribbing their entire life. Don't follow their footsteps or you too will be in the same gutter. Mark my words!'

'Okay, okay.' I knew there was no point discussing all this with him any further. 'What was the saying, by the way?'

'Time and new girlfriends mend the pain. And who the hell has time in this fast-paced world? Even food is fast food. Everything is readymade now. So are girlfriends. Get committed and sleep with her ...'

'Okay, okay. I got your point.'

'Great. See, this is greatness. Don't get involved in matters of the heart and in these stupid things like trust, understanding, and all that funda. It never works and they will friend-zone you. Would you like that?'

'Certainly not!'

'Then don't stalk anyone on Facebook. It doesn't work,' he sneered.

'Ah, I am not stalking anyone.'

'Don't worry. I was just kidding. Will share other secrets later.'

'Secrets?'

'Yes. There is an art to impress girls.'

'Okay. Great.' And he left the room. His words encouraged me and that was the first time I decided that I would go nowhere else but Delhi.

I walked ahead. Wherever my head turned I saw beauties and slender bodies whizzing past me like scent. As if the air had turned pink and lavender. The road was lit up in electric radiance. In front of me I could see a sea of girls tugging at my desperate heart like a wild wave. My eyes grew wider and at that moment it was even possible that they would pop out and I wouldn't be surprised. Reality suddenly made me hopeful. I could see shapely, waxed legs rising up to bodies in full bloom. Some were in shorts, some in miniskirts, some even in hot pants. One could look at them for centuries and wonder if God was the perfect recycler! Something so beautiful coming straight out of a man's rib? Impossible. As I floated through the sea of lithe, petite bodies in wonder and awe, one of them brushed past me. It was difficult to say whether she was trying to display the straps of her bra sticking out of her top or if she wanted the viewer to focus on the loose top that by some rare luck managed to cover it up. Similar girls brushed behind, and their faces almost became one as my eyes darted from one to the other. I could only see legs and breasts! I realized that Utsav wasn't wrong with his bang-bang story. It was indeed true.

The painted faces, the lined eyes, the scent of rosewater wafting through the air reminded me of Utsav's words. How the world starts and ends in the beauty parlour for them! The first thing they do in the morning is to break a flaming mirror that tells them that they aren't beautiful and rush to a parlour like mad dogs hunting for bones. I was finding it harder to believe. As I moved ahead the flock of girls seemed to grow in size, as if the world had suddenly burst into Eden right after the apocalypse. At that moment I honestly sought someone who could pinch me hard and tell me it wasn't a dream after all. I told my heart, 'Control kar saale!'

I passed through the crowd as my eyes speared through each girl, X-raying each from top to bottom. The number of girls seemed to increase unnaturally, almost as if they were viral. I couldn't have enough. By that time I had checked out and X-rayed so many of them that I hadn't seen in the last five years of my life. The word 'sexy' was definitely an understatement. Or maybe it was only invented for them. It is here that the etymological origin of that word lay. The universe had contorted, merged, and shrunk to Connaught Place that day. The rhythm of the earth could be felt in their grace, the way they moved and carried themselves. How could everyone be so elegant and graceful? Maybe the way we had extra classes for Sanskrit, these girls too had classes to *sex* themselves up enough when they grew up!

I stopped near a showroom and glanced in. It was full with customers and whoever came out of the store had at least one bag. The reason, of course, was the salesgirl. I found her inordinately beautiful. I thought of going inside but I must buy at least one thing. I must avoid looking stupid in front of her and make a khichdi out of myself, the way I always do. I called up Utsav.

'Hey! How's Delhi, man? Enjoying yourself?' asked Utsav.

'It's beautiful. And I am standing amidst the sexiest girls of India.'

He started laughing. 'What did I tell you? All are smoking hot, aren't they?'

'You were right about break-ups and commitments. Who would stick to one girl and why? More so when every other chick is a bomb!'

'Yes. And you will get them automatically. Only thing is, you need to spend some money. The rest will happen in its own pace or probably faster than you even imagined.'

'Yes. I can believe that now.'

'No doubt your tips and secrets give 100 per cent guarantee.' And we both cracked up.

After wrecking my head over getting one single good girl I did end up meeting an English major chick from Hindu. She came round the corner of Turtle Café and I sat with her for hours. By that time I had forgotten the salesgirl I had seen some weeks back. Every girl was worth falling for so it hardly made a difference. Our chats seemed to be never ending, not only in person but also over the phone. I was happy to offer her solutions on how to cope with her broken family and how she should be calm though her parents fought almost every day. At first I thought things were going just the way I wanted. She called me every day and I went running to help her. But when the judgment day came and I professed my love to her, she ended up saying that she had always considered me as a good friend and couldn't think of me on those lines. I was not only upset but frustrated. I had made so much of emotional investment already. I felt broken and called up Gaurav. He seemed to understand the low tone of my voice.

'So, friend-zoned again?' he asked. I could hear his sneering tone but I was used to it.

'Yes,' I said sadly.

'Dude, I seriously think you're jinxed. Some nutcase in school must have fallen for you and must have cast something on you and you still carry that curse! I mean, honestly, how come you fail every time and nothing works out?'

'Why does this happen with me every time? This time I didn't make any mistake. In fact, I called her and talked about her every problem.'

'Wait. You talked about her problems and don't you say that you tried to preach to her?' he asked inquisitively.

'Yes. What's wrong with that? I tried to support her.'

'Well done, my boy. I understand now why you get friend-zoned every time. Do one thing. Open a girl's problem-solution centre. And start charging a fee for this because you are anyway not going to get girls. You will get some cash to spend on yourself or at least for your phone recharge.'

'What do you mean?'

'What is the point of calling her whenever she wanted to talk to you and why the hell did you solve her every problem and listen to her?'

'I don't know but what's wrong with that?'

'Nothing.'

'Then?'

'See, a girl needs a guy who can solve her problems, listen to her all the time, and can talk to someone who listens to her without expecting anything. That's what you were doing for her. If she was getting all this from you, then, I mean, why would she make you her boyfriend? Girls never make such guys their boyfriends.'

'But what's wrong with me? I am good looking, I care for her, and in fact love her.'

'See, girls are impressed by guys who remain mysterious to them, who don't go to them so easily. Once you are available to them all the time, they will take you for granted and will dump you in the friend zone.'

'But isn't that the ironic? I mean, it's a good thing, right? Always available for her whenever she wants to talk to you and needs support from you. I mean, how come I would lose importance?'

'Because you are stupid! Logic doesn't work here, my friend. Okay? Let me give you an example. You have immense respect for Shah Rukh Khan. Right?'

'Yes. He is a superstar.'

'Right. And suppose you talk to him on a daily basis, would you care for him and respect him in the same way as you do now?'

It was a tricky question and I remained silent.

'You won't. It's human nature, you see. You never give importance to stuff that you have in hand easily or that which is always with you. You don't have to strive for it or be desperate about it. It's the same with you and girls. When they know that they can have you any time they want, and for any goddamn problem they are in, you'd end up being the saviour why would they want you or, for that matter, crave you? They would, in fact crave someone who isn't easily available to them, who flirts with them but doesn't make it explicitly clear to them that he's gonna be with them no matter what and in all odd hours. Girls never want someone who would be a problem-solver and who would keep on preaching to them on each and every topic. Got my point?'

'But this is unfair. A relationship doesn't work on candlelight dinners but on trust, understanding, and mutual affection.'

'Great thought. Do one thing. Build a time machine and travel to a century earlier and try to use your funda there. Got it?'

'I don't know. Something is seriously wrong with girls

out here. They will chase some stupid guys who will talk all sorts of nonsense with them, that too without an iota of knowledge, and flirt with them with as many dumb jokes possible. Then, of course, their usual tactic: have the girls sit behind them on bikes and apply the brakes just at the right junction and moment so that they can have the delight of "pressings"!'

'And this is exactly what a girl likes, dude! A guy makes her laugh, gives her gifts. They are so soft that they would rather get impressed with a teddy bear than with a Salman Rushdie book that you carry on a date.'

'Yeah! True. To add to this, something is also seriously wrong with my destiny. Hey, you know how to read the Tarot, right? Would you read the Tarot for me and check my fate?'

'Okay, I'll do that. You send me three questions and I will let you know. Before that, I will tell you once secret. The faster you bring a girl closer to yourself, probably to bed, the closer girls get to you.'

'Wow! Wonderful. Here I am getting friend-zoned each time and you are suggesting that I go to bed with them. Are you drunk? I mean, I talk to you because I always consider you to talk sense but now you are completely out of your mind.'

'Okay. Don't believe me. Why don't you try to hang out with a girl in Delhi? Long-term relationships don't work out much and talking on the phone doesn't leave much impact on her mind. Delhi has hot and sexy girls. Try your chance. And who knows, you might get a chance to take one to bed too.' He smirked. I felt like punching his face.

'Wow. I mean, how? I just need to go to the road and when I find any beautiful girl and I should start talking to her, isn't it? And then the slaps following will surely lose their count.'

'No. I mean, visit new places. Join some club. Or go to pubs. These are the best places to meet new girls. And yes, before going there, do one more thing. Get a facial and all and yes, change your hairstyle. Your current hairstyle is perfect for an interview or job but get a sexy look.'

'Which style?'

'How do I know? Visit a parlour and they will take care of your look. Don't sound boring and look boring.'

'Yes, boss.' And we both started laughing.

5

ANIS UNISEX PARLOUR. SUCH a contradictory name. Perhaps this is how people in Delhi imbibed metrosexuality into words and attitudes. It was the weekend and in my quest for a better parlour, I landed at Anis. On that line of the road I could see many other parlours as well but then I decided on Anis, speculating on its interesting name and noticing the number of people flocking inside.

I pushed open the glass door and the strong scent of musk pushed its way up my nostrils. A girl stood in the doorway against the portrait of a shirtless chap flaunting his extra-wavy hair and muscles. She was the receptionist and looked quite inviting. 'How may I help you, sir?' She had a thick, accented voice. She smiled into a perfect crescent, showing a radiant set of teeth. I gulped. My feet were giving away.

As I began to speak, I felt my tongue rolling against my palate and ended up fumbling. After a moment of silence I took control and managed to speak, 'I am here for a haircut and a facial.'

She smiled. Probably thinking that I looked like another desperate wannabe!

Then she said, 'Okay, great! I would request you to wait here for a few minutes. All our hairdressers are serving other customers.'

'Okay.' She showed me down a well-lit corridor. The walls were pasted with posters of men and women with similar extra-wavy hair and showing the right muscles and curves. I walked to the corner seat lounge. All other seats at the other end of the waiting lounge were occupied with girls. Almost all of them looked the same. Or perhaps it was my eyes. All of them were sexy with glistening legs. I cursed under my breath, 'What the fuck! What more do they need. Why at have they come here at all?' It was absurd. All were decked to perfection and looked as if they had already had whatever nose job or pout job was to be done. Honestly, girls in Delhi have nothing else to do and are obsessed with beautifying themselves. At a certain point I did contemplate on falling in love with such a girl who would spend twenty hours of the day in the parlour itself but then maybe I didn't want that. I was just being desperate; as Gaurav said, I needed to get laid, that's all. The sofa in the lounge was so soft that I almost slipped into its depths and it made a squeaky sound. Some girls turned around and smiled. I smiled back meekly, thinking that I had lost my chance with any of them. I must be looking like a dumbass!

When I had had enough of staring at the girls, I lay there sinking deeper into the seat and ruminating like a hungry cow. I had nothing to do at this hour and the line was never-ending. The customers were not ready to move out of their seats. After every facial another pedicure was lined up and then some steam therapy. Spa, yes, that's what they call it. It was taking an eternity. I tried to pick up a magazine and flip through its pages. It didn't interest me in the least. Just then a guy came out from inside one of the chambers. He had a chiselled face with muscles cutting into his electric-red T-shirt. His face glittered like ice and for a second I thought that men could be beautiful too. Suddenly I became self-conscious and tilted my head to steal a glance at my own face in the mirror on the side. It was the same boring face, with a lopsided arc for a mouth. I looked dark, with the soot of all of Delhi pasted on my skin. And on top of that, the blackheads on and around my nose made me look pitiable in my own eyes. Seriously, I needed a big makeover. Big with a capital 'B'. Gaurav was right. Why would girls like me, of all people, when there are such studs flocking around the city wearing ripped T-shirts and zooming off on bikes. I had bad inferiority complex and was sulking.

I was called after about ten minutes more. I went inside. It was a huge chamber with life-sized mirrors on the walls.

The guy who had called me in gestured for me to sit on a large chair. I could almost sink into it and never come out. He started with tying a band on my forehead and pulled it tight. I thought I would crack my neck. But then I saw almost everyone—men and women alike—had similar bandanas tied around their heads. It was so that the cream from the facial would not seep into the hair. He took a thick dab of L'Oreal facial cream in his palms and applied it gently on my face. In the mirror in front of me I could see girls being given similar massages. I had the urge to get up from my seat and join the masseur as his assistant. At least that way I could strike up a conversation with one of the girls. But after a moment I felt like a desperate fool. As if someone had inflated a balloon to its full size and then left its mouth open to a miserable puncture. After some time he stopped the rotating movements of his hands on my face and I could instead feel a vibrating corrugated plate on my cheeks making a strange buzzing sound. It felt as if little insects were nibbling at my skin. I now understood the secret of beauty for men and women alike. It was far more important to *look* beautiful than to *be* beautiful.

After the facial was done, another guy, this time with a silky black apron tied around his waist, came and held my head in the the crook of his arm. He held my chin and cradled it in a different direction to see how 'hairy' I was, at least that is what I assumed then. And then gave a click of the tongue as if struck with the knowledge of the secret formula with which he could change me into Adonis overnight. He brought an iPad and asked me to flip through the different hairstyles on offer. But I couldn't decide on what I wanted. All of them looked alien to me. As if any of those hairdos would suit any Tom, Dick, and Harry but when it came to me it would certainly suck. He then took charge with a sardonic smile and started running his fingers along his scissors. I murmured 'Bhagwan' under my breath, apprehensive in case the hairstyle went wrong. It took him over forty minutes to ultimately showcase his talent and flaunt it with utter indifference. After all, it was a trick he performed daily. 'There you go,' he said. 'I almost always know how to make a star out of a cucumber.' 'What?' I asked, thinking I had misheard. 'Never mind,' he muttered, and glided like a ghost in black into another direction, merging with the crowd of anxious customers. 'Never mind,' I repeated to myself and looked into the mirror. A boy came in with a big brush and cleaned all the hair from the piece of silky cloth that still covered my front. He brushed my neck and blasted hot air from a hairdryer onto my face to rid me of the remaining small hairs stuck to me. Only then could I see my face in the mirror. I looked different, there was no doubt about it. I looked perfect. The sides were trimmed with precision and my sideburns gleamed like sharp blades. My face looked longish. I no longer looked like a 'bhaiya-ji'. I thanked God while I headed to the reception to pay up.

I proudly came out of the inner chamber, looking at the girls and passing conceited smiles to them. They seemed to notice me too. My heart did a jig inside and I felt my balloon inflating confidently once again. It couldn't be punctured anymore. But then there is always one or the other shock awaiting me after a period of relief and comfort. This time it was at the reception table as the receptionist handed me the bill.

'What? 3000 bucks? What for?'

'Sir, you can check our price list. It was for the haircut, facial, bleaching, and massage. We can offer you a 10 per cent discount. Corporate discount. Are you working or a college student?'

'What do you think I'd be?' I gave her a mocking interrogatory look.

'When you came here earlier, you looked like a working professional but now, you look like a college student.' I sensed some insult against me.

'What do you mean? I am working. And this is my office card.' I showed her the card. She seemed satisfied then. Rs 3000 was the only way out at that moment. I felt like digging the notes out and throwing them at her face. That would teach her and her staff some manners. I pulled out my wallet from my pocket and checked the notes in it. It contained only had Rs 200 and some change. She craned her neck doubtfully to look into my wallet. I turned around and flipped out my debit card. I handed it to her and waited at the counter. For a second I wanted to spit in her face. I felt extremely unnerved and disturbed. She, however, swiped my card mechanically and pulled out the receipt. I signed it and stormed out. It was only the beginning, I realized. There was a pit of guilt inside my stomach. I had literally splurged and emptied my pockets! What had I got myself into?

6

NOW I HAD TO JUMP into the scene and the scene was to be in one of those pubs that Gaurav had asked me to go to. In the circuit of my friends or my office no one knew much about pubs in Delhi. At least I had not heard any of them discussing what they did over the weekends on Monday mornings. I assumed most of them were either boring and had nothing else to do in life other than sleep or that they were just as unlucky as I me. There was, however, a guy named Mayank who was friendly with me and he used the Delhi lingo of 'Wassup dude!' quite often. I thought of asking him if he knew of such places. I asked him at lunch if he would like to accompany me to the pub. He looked at me wide-eyed and asked, 'Have you ever been to a pub or, for that matter, a discotheque?' I gulped uneasily and said, 'No. Never, actually.' He smiled serenely and patted my back as if he had suddenly become my guru. 'Doncha worry, dude. Hum hain na!'

That night itself we landed up at the pub Q-Bar. All I could see was a long queue serpentining its way to the road. I asked Mayank if we had to join the same queue to which he just nodded and gestured me to follow. I saw girls in the skimpiest of shorts and skirts clinging to big, muscled guys like snakes coiled around a pole. The ratio was funny. The bigger the guy, the smaller the girl. Two bouncers stood like sentinels at the doorway, busy checking the people letting them enter. A nerdy-looking guy stood there too, checking the entries and noting down the names and identities on a clipboard.

As we reached closer, I looked up at the board hung above the doors.

COUPLE ENTRY—FREE
SINGLE—Rs1000/- GIRLS—FREE

I was taken aback. It was absurd. Couple entry was free and a single was charged 1000 bucks! Wasn't that preposterous, I asked Mayank.

'Dude, doncha know, girls and couples are supposed to be the centre of attraction of any pub you go to. Otherwise any lallu-panju would be allowed in, you see. And who would come to check them out?'

'Yeah, right.' I gave a sardonic smile. And these people talk about equality in this country. I was thinking about this when the bouncer suddenly held my wrist and punched a stamp just below my palm.

'What is this?' I asked Mayank.

'A confirmation that you have paid.'

'It reminds me of brothels in movies where flowers are showered on you when you enter and here is this stamp. Modern approach, huh!'

'Dude, why are you bothering with all this, man? Come inside. You'll find apsaras waiting for you,' he said excitedly. But I was more excited than him.

We walked inside. The loud music was ripping my eardrums and there were flashing neon lights. There were many couples and almost everyone was dancing madly, without any rhythm. Some people were sitting on couches in corners of the pub. My eyes were searching for hot girls and I wasn't disappointed. The pub was full of ravishing girls who were dancing, some with a glass in their hands. Singles like me were ogling them.

I could never understand the logic of such dancing. I mean, what fun is it at all? Dance like a sensible person if at all you want to dance. The 'dancers' were making lewd, jerky movements as if struck by electric lightning and were gyrating without any rhythm or beat. Was this what was called dance? Was this the reason they all came to the disco—so that they could move so repulsively?

We stayed on the stage in the centre for some time and then Mayank pulled me towards the bar. He ordered a glass of rum for himself and asked me what I wanted to have. When I said nothing, examining the non-alcoholic drinks menu, the bartender intervened and asked if I'd like to go with a glass of vodka with a shot of lime cordial to ease myself. I avoided his question. I found that even the mocktails were overpriced. I politely refused, patting my back pocket and thinking of the 3000 bucks I had thoughtlessly spent the other day. My only consolation was the fact that I had a hairstyle that matched many of those muscled hunks sitting on couches with the girls. If not muscles, I had hair like theirs. It was a relief! At least the money I had spent did some good. I looked at Mayank sipping his drink and thumping his feet to the music.

He turned towards me and said, 'They're free.'

'What?'

'Drinks.'

'Really?'

'Yes. The entry fee includes drinks.'

'Oh. Great, then I will have a mocktail,' I said to the bartender.

'Which one?'

'Any of them. Whichever is your favourite.'

'Try this,' and he started preparing a glass for me.

'Mayank, tell me one thing. I was wondering how these people manage this pub. I mean, Rs 1000 for everything, including drinks! How do they make a profit?'

'Dude, are ya kidding me? What has got into your head? Don't talk like a bloody lunatic,' He looked at me disdainfully. His lips were wet with rum and he was almost on the verge of spitting a mouthful into my face. 'I tell you, you're one nutcase! Why at all do ya have to bother how they manage the pub or how much profit they're gonna make? If you're so interested about calculating their profits, why don't you join them as their general manager? Or you might as well give your CV to them and they may hire you rightaway. That way you could also ogle girls from the counter and keep ogling them your whole life!'

I felt embarrassed at his outburst.

'Arre yaar, I just asked generally. Why are you getting angry at me? Okay, sorry. I was just curious.'

That was really a stupid question and I had just asked the wrong question to the wrong person. I mean, why did it even occur to me? I scolded myself and thought for a moment if I was really the odd one out. I could never be in a situation without analysing its unnecessary details. I must get rid of this way of thinking. I shook my head and started checking out the girls dancing on the floor. All of them were pretty and I was desperate owl. I wished I could turn my head 180 degrees!

Then suddenly there was a sweet voice from behind me, 'Hey!' I immediately turned towards it.

There stood a lovely, curvy girl. She was clad in a shiny golden skirt and a fawn top which revealed her deep cleavage. A bra strap was carelessly displayed across her collarbone. I wondered why so many girls here showed off their undergarments. Was it an open invitation to men? But I couldn't risk ruining Mayank's mood again by asking him this. Also, I didn't want to lose my own chance with this pretty girl. She wore heavy make-up that highlighted her cheekbones and her lips were painted deep red. Her large, expressive eyes were lined with mascara, and she had mid-length straight hair. Her arms and legs were waxed and glowed in the dim, changing light. She must have taken hours to dress up and would have spent her entire afternoon in the parlour. What else did girls do here except spend their time and money in the parlour. Though guys too spent half their day in the gym.

The girl extended her hands towards Mayank and I could see an ornate ring glinting on her middle finger. She almost stole my breath away and I felt my chest getting heavy.

I looked at Mayank. His eyes sparkled.

'Hey, Aleena,' and he shook her hand. 'What a pleasant surprise! After a long time.' It was a pleasant shock for me as well.

'Mayank knows her? What the hell! How does he know such a sexy girl? He doesn't even look all that great.'

My reverie broke when Mayank introduced her to me.

'Aleena, this is my friend Sameer.'

She smiled her killer smile and extended her hand.

'Hi, Sam.'

'Sam'? Whoa, that was fast. But it felt nice. In fact, every word she uttered felt like honey flowing from her lips. I had to secure my chance before the moment passed. I grabbed her hands. I suddenly thought of Gaurav as his ghost hovered in front of my eyes against the walls of the bar. He seemed to smile and I felt his words turning into reality. Beautiful girls in beautiful pubs! Her hands were soft and I could, in that moment, drown myself in her eyes. I immediately started thinking of the future. We would be married and have twenty kids and she would still look as ravishing as now. Though our handshake had lasted not more than five seconds, I had already devised plans with her for eternity. She demurely pulled out of my grip and smiled mischievously. I smiled back meekly and felt like a physics experiment gone wrong.

'Hi Aleena.' And the conversation stopped there itself while I pondered on what to say further. My mouth went dry. She stroked my shoulders and went and sat near Mayank. They were soon engaged in their own chit-chat and I stood there helplessly.

What do I do now? How do I carry forward the conversation? Should I ask her to dance? Would that do any good? I thought I was going crazy. But I had never learnt how to dance. What would I do with her? I felt like a fool and as if the wires to my brain were cut midway. I was embarrassed and shrunk within myself like a mole.

Gaurav, fuck you, man! You just told me to groom myself and go to a pub but never told me what to do after that, how to introduce myself to a girl and what to say beyond a 'hi'. I was stranded midway. Perhaps Gaurav wasn't confident that I would be able to pass through the test of entering a pub and meeting a sexy girl. I was busy contemplating on my disabilities and cursing Gaurav under my breath and didn't even realize that my dreams breaking up just in front of me. Aleena was joined by another muscled hunk, whose shirt, it seemed, would tear any moment if he flexed his arms. She told Mayank that he was her new boyfriend and that they had met just a week back. I felt the same balloon puncturing itself with a small swoosh somewhere deep inside. I felt like running away and escaping into the woodwork and never coming out of it. I felt like a failure.

As usual, nothing else happened after that in the pub. I felt morose and couldn't say a single word. It was midnight and I had nothing to do. On reaching home, I looked at myself in the mirror and scanned as many defects I could locate on my face, from the oddly placed mole to the jagged vein running down my jaw. And then, when I grew tired of my self-reproach, I shrugged off my T-shirt and flung it on the and buried my face into the pillow. I felt miserable. And with that misery stinging deep in my heart I went off to sleep.

In the weeks that passed, I thought of clearing my mind and considering my stupidity. This was once again a temporary phase of realization that came and went like a gust of strong wind that knocks you off your feet. But once it is gone you would rather move out to the window and have a smoke, preparing to set the curtains on fire when this phase next hits you.

I switched on my laptop and logged in to an online book site. I was on an overdrive of ambition. I scanned the site with eyes as big as buttons for books that would give me the perfect entry to the best MBA course. But as I did so, I felt my drive wearing out to lethargy. I started checking out books like *101 Ways of Mending a Broken Heart* as also *10 Easy Ways of Winning the Girl*. I ended up ordering them.

The next day, when the delivery boy landed up at my doorstep carrying the parcels, I thrust the cash into his hands and tore off the wrapper. I had finished fifty pages by the evening but the book was all about finding flaws in myself, and gave a truckload of superfluous advice, from going out to movies with friends to clubbing and dancing with other girls at night, concluding with a section on one-night stands.

For the next few days, a wave of enthusiasm hit me again and I tried to get on track, checking websites having their panel discussions on entering the best college. And doing the kind of research to ensure my 99.99 percentile in the CAT exam at least this time. But the more I thought about this, the more I found myself drifting into random conversations with random people on Facebook the whole night long, listening to their stupid tragedies and sharing some of mine, fictionalizing bits and pieces. Days went by and weeks too, until one morning I was pulled up with a real 'wake-up' call.

The next day, I woke up to the violent vibrations of my phone. I had been sound asleep. It must have been vibrating for quite a long time. I opened an eye and checked the number. It was from Dad.

'Hello,' I almost managed to croak.

'Hello, Sameer? You are still sleeping?'

'Yes. It's Sunday.'

'So what?'

'Dad, tell me what is the matter? I slept very late night yesterday.'

'It's ten in the morning. Late night? Why? Were you studying for your MBA entrance exams? How is your preparation going on?'

'It's going good,' I lied. I knew that Dad wasn't going to ask any more questions it.

'Very good. It's the only hope for us. You know it is getting more and more difficult to get through to a good institute. I don't feel good telling you all these things, beta, but you are sensible and can understand the difficulties and strife that we have gone through. Though you are the youngest, I have treated you as my eldest. You know, the house is in a shambles. On top of that, the owner is that asking us to vacate it as soon as possible. My other worry is that I stay here in a different district and your

Bhaiya–Bhabhi stay someplace else. Your mother and sister are really alone. I do not want any adversity to strike them, you see. You understand, beta.' He sounded defeated and I felt sorry for what he was going through. 'We now only hope that once you get through a good MBA in a good institute we can then think of mending all our troubles. Plus your sister too needs to marry off soon. I hope it is a matter only of two to three years more and then perhaps everything will be in order. Your mother too thinks and hopes the same, beta.'

I knew this was a serious issue and I was the only one who could solve everyone's problems. For the last few months, Dad hadn't received his full salary and now they needed to vacate the house. It was annoying and I felt burdened with guilt and remorse at the same time. I wondered how they would solve the problem. I couldn't possibly go to my hometown and help them find a new house. I had just joined work and wouldn't get leave under any circumstances. My sister's marriage was also getting delayed, and that, of course, was another cause of worry for my parents. And I was wasting my time chasing girls like a mad, inglorious dog. I felt ashamed of myself and more so for wasting so much of money when I should be concentrating on helping my family. Dad's voice broke something in my heart and I felt it melting like a heavy slab of ice. I choked and felt my eyes welling up. The thought of unrequited love too pierced me bit by bit and perhaps that is why I acted so desperate, so restless. Everything had escaped me in this quest for pleasure which for some time I thought to be the ultimate portal to love. I must not waste myself on such volatile emotions anymore. I was the only hope for my parents. There was nothing else that I could think of at that moment.

He continued, 'What would happen on this petty salary? It's just enough for a person to barely make his ends meet. Food and lodging, that's all. Delhi is an expensive metro city. Rs 500 is like Rs 100. The moment you get out of the house the money vanishes into thin air. Everything is so exorbitantly priced. When I had come a decade back to Delhi, Rs 100 was like Rs 10. And now look at it.' It had been quite long since Dad spoke his heart out. But whenever he did, I never interrupted him. And whenever he did, he always spoke about his old days in Delhi. His words were actually not meant to remind me of my responsibilities. He, in fact, always felt that I would be the one who would understand him even if the world didn't. Hence, whenever he spoke to me, I would be overcome by a deep longing to fulfil all the troubles that my parents were going through at the moment and to find the best way to resolve them.

'When do you have your CAT exam?' he asked.

'It's on 22nd October.'

'Just three more months. Work very hard, beta. It's been a really long time since we have stayed together in one house and if you pass the exam, I can, for once, rest with the feeling that there is nothing else I need to do to hold up the responsibilities for my family. I could pass them on to you.' I could hear his breath going shallow over the phone and I really wanted to give him a hug at that moment, comfort him. 'I did try to build a new house, you know, beta. But then it just didn't happen. At Rs 40,000 a month, building a ghar is difficult to manage. Yet we educated you and did the best for you. It doesn't concern me as much but it's your mother for whom I really remain worried. She hasn't been keeping well of late, you know that. She longs for a house of her own. And now that I am here away from her and your sister, I somehow cannot bring things together and tie them up. You get me, beta?'

'I understand, Dad. Tell me one thing, isn't there a chance to get a transfer in the same district?'

'I am also waiting for the same. I hope they will transfer all the officers before the election but who knows. You know how the Bihar government works. Last week I went to Patna and bribed the officers with Rs 5000 to transfer me in our district so that it would be good for your mom.'

'Hmm.' I couldn't say anything.

'Son, you are our only hope. We have waited two decades for things to fall in place. Don't let us wait for long. Work hard. Crack the MBA and get a good job.'

'Yes, Dad. I will.' And he disconnected the line.

My heart filled on listening to my father after such a long

time. I felt guilty and at the same time something shifted inside me, knotting up uneasily. Tears welled up in my eyes thinking of him. He was fifty-seven, greying slowly and losing his strength. Yet he cooked on his own, laid his bed in that lonely place and in that lonely little quarter and slept without a fan in this scorching heat. God knows what he ate after coming back tired from office. He worked day and night to ensure the best for our house and the best for my mother and sister and till this date had hardly complained about anything. I never saw him getting angry or being an escapist. In comparison, I thought, what did I require? I had a roof over my head, I never had to cook my own food, and neither did I suffer from monetary problems as such. I had everything and yet I wasted my time and energy on stupid things like grooming myself and chasing girls. That was utterly unnecessary. I was not the kind of guy who would do such things to merely impress a girl or worse, be a despo. And even if I ended up getting someone who would love me back, would I really call it love? Would it not wear out and become only a remnant of what we assume to love? It's all an illusion. True love doesn't happen like that. It's a pity I allowed myself to be deluded. If someone loved me then she would love me not because of the way I look or because of the way I groom myself. She would love me because of the person I am and the virtues I carry within. For the moment, I guessed I should just stop thinking about all this nonsense and focus entirely on clearing my MBA and getting into one of the top-notch colleges.

7

I COULDN'T REMEMBER THE EXACT moment I had decided on an MBA as my career path but I do remember that it was Steve Jobs who fascinated me beyond measure. It was his innovation and his die-hard attitude about what he created that somehow made me feel that in the world of numbers, everything could be sold. And that money ultimately harboured more money. One doesn't need to belong to any elitist society to make a difference in this world. It is innovation and sheer hard work that does that. It was the year when he had come up with the iPhone that I decided that I would try to become someone like him, as I passionately waited for its launch. Moreover, doing an MBA was the easiest way possible, as an MBA in finance led the highest-paying jobs. Thinking of all this, I had appeared for the CAT in the last year of college as well but ended up scoring an 85 percentile only. I realized I had to work harder and that there was certainly a long way to go.

I looked at the new books I had ordered online, scattered around my bed almost in a ring. I wondered what exactly I was doing with my life with all these books on relationships, tips on improving one's chances with a girl, or finding the right girl in a pub or a bar. I stared into space listlessly. Cobwebs had darkened the ceiling of my room and perhaps my heart too was darkened with hopeless dreams. Such things would do no good, I realized. If I carried on like this, then I couldn't possibly clear the MBA entrance or any exams, for that matter. What mattered most in life? I must decide on my priorities first. Mom and Dad had given me more than their life to get me to this place, to this very place I was at the moment. How could I jeopardize it by committing myself to stupidity and that too in desperation? Hadn't I known that desperation was the worst reason to fall in love, for every flame dies out one day? It was such an absurd situation to think of—what I had become in the mindless chase for girls. I remembered my night in the bar and imagined more such nights to come. I was filled with shame and felt like burrowing into the walls of my room. I felt them closing in on me and needed to get out of the room. It wasn't actually too late. I had come to Delhi and seen its true face—grotesque and selfish. Now I only needed to be indifferent to it and concentrate on what could best be mended. I picked up the books and carried them to the stack of newspapers. Next time the raddiwala came around, I had to hand the entire stack over to him. At least I would get some money and with that I would treat myself to a good meal. That was much better than running behind girls. And now it was time to order more books for my MBA studies. It was time to mend my ways. As I kept thinking, my mind drifted and wandered to various planes and worlds, thinking of what life had in store for me.

Was it true that I wouldn't ever have love in this life? I would remain a man of unrequited love. Would Gaurav's words about me in the Tarot cards turn out to be true?

Sitting in my balcony, I thought about it for perhaps the thousandth time in six years. And definitely the five hundredth time in the last five years. Looking up at the sky, I let the question filter through the grain of my being and wondered about all that would follow. The sun had slipped behind the clouds yet it was hot. The sky had turned grey and the clouds had become thick balls, tossing and turning like the dead in their graves. I could hear water dripping into a bucket but apart from that, there was silence. Inside, I felt everything folding and merging into a tiny, silent dot. Only my mind wasn't quiet. It would take time, I thought. Suddenly it was dusk and darkness enveloped me. I was back to where I had been two years back. My desires would bring me pain and despair and nothing else. I was the kind of person who believed in committing to memory every single note of happiness and never let myself be despondent on the past. But as I recollected the series of events since the time I had landed in this damned city, I felt I was changing. I was becoming more and more depressed. And that was precisely because I was chasing the wrong dream, and giving myself to the wrong sorts of people. My perception of the world had been tainted and I had turned blind to what life could offer. It all made me feel helpless and dark inside. If I didn't take charge of the situation soon, it would perhaps kill me. I could not let that happen. Sadness acts like slow poison and I had to devise a way to get out of it. I had to make my life lighter. And that wouldn't happen if I left myself in the throes of desperation.

They say that behind romantic desperation is an old flame burning the innards of the soul. I ruminated on my own old flame. It was years and I had neglected to reopen and deal with that wound which lay in some dark crevice of my heart. Her name was Tanvi. I knew I was getting into the bog of becoming an emotional fool but she seemed to be my only hope. I hadn't dwelt on her as well as the memories gone by, thinking that love left untouched wears out like dark, dissolving paint. Till the time I wasn't emotionally involved with anyone I had no such mindless troubles in my life but, as they say, once drowned in love, one has already plunged as far into the ocean as one can. I couldn't erase her out of my life and start life anew. I sometimes wished I could roll back time like a dirty paper and erase everything that had the capacity to haunt me.

I could see nothing beyond the murky darkness. I returned to my room and lay down on the couch next to the door but the memories didn't let me sleep though I tried to force Tanvi's image away from my mind.

I had only thought of a hand to hold and nursed hopes of togetherness. I don't think I had asked for much. And now I was back to the terrible juncture where life seemed to begin. Everything came back to the same point of struggle.

I dragged myself to office the next day and saw Mayank working at his desk. I did not bother walking up to him and telling him about the burden I had been enduring since the last night and since Dad's call the previous morning. I felt miserable and zombie-like inside the office. Another colleague, Taufeeq, had become close to me since the last few days. He observed my sullenness and came up to me to ask if anything was wrong. For the sake of courtesy, I gave him a wry smile and said nothing had actually gone wrong. He moved on, walking into the other direction without probing further. At lunchtime he came to me as I was sipping on a cold drink, staring into space. He insisted I tell him what was bothering me. I thought of opening up to him and telling him what was biting me from inside. I complained about Delhi to him and how I had got into my desperate situation. How I had ended up in the bar and made a fool of myself. I told him about my luck with girls and about home as well. That I was nothing but sad at the end of everything and was tired of trying.

'Dude. It's not that tough, but you need to know that there is a way to impress girls. You just can't go up to her and ask her out on a date. That's stupid,' Taufeeq said.

'Yes, I know. Then what am I supposed to do?'

'I'll tell you something. You need to follow some protocol.'

'Protocol? You mean to say that there are certain rules and by following those you can impress girl?'

'Yes, unless you are a funky badass and can convince a girl to come out with you a date that easily. But I know you aren't that type of a guy at all. You won't and you can't.'

'See. I have always thought that a relationship requires care, patience, understanding, and trust. Why should I change myself just to impress girls? Isn't it stupid?'

'I agree. But whatever you have mentioned happens only in a utopian land. Trust and all. You tried all this, showed care and affection to a girl, and what did you get in return? It's difficult to understand the mind of a girl, dude. The moment you start being polite and extra-good to them, start discussing their personal problems and give them advice, they start considering you as a friend and never want to commit to a romantic relationship. They actually need someone who can take them for a ride, and that includes the literal too. Who doesn't like adventure, tell me? I am telling you, they otherwise only end up saying,

"I have never thought about it. I thought we are friends. I consider you to be a very good friend of mine. You are such a nice guy and you will get a beautiful and nice girl."'

'That's true. I am tired of listening to this,' I sighed.

'Yes, that's what I am saying. Just tell me one thing—why wouldn't they get into a relationship with you when they find you to be a nice person? Why? They don't want a nice boyfriend. Isn't that all bullshit?'

'Hmm. They say they don't feel a spark with me.'

'What? That's ridiculous. What do you think? That a romantic movie is going on that someone will play the violin and its music would be the signal for your love to arrive? And what else? It's so funny to see them. First they will get hooked to some bad guy and when the guy cheats on them then they come to you crying, saying that all boys are the same. Just think. In the first place, why did they go to those bad boys if they knew it all? It only means that the saying is right: good boys get heaven and bad boys get women.'

I started laughing.

He nodded. 'Believe me, it's all bullshit.'

I remained silent.

'Don't try to be nice to a girl. Don't remain available for her. Don't call her regularly. If she calls you, don't pick up the call on the first ring, let her call you a few times before you pick up, and don't say sorry and all. Just talk for a few seconds and disconnect, saying something important has come up. Be mysterious. It works.' Are you following me?' he asked.

'Yes. I am following you.'

Probably he was right. I was nice to everyone and gave them time despite my busy schedule. And they took me for granted.

Shagun sighed and grimaced. She kept wondered at the desperation of the man she was married to. She loved this man. But such twisted tales seemed to belong to a different person altogether. If this story had been told to her by her husband, she perhaps would never have believed him. Even at the cost of jeopardizing their relationship. But this diary was not only proof but a written validation by the very person she was reading about. For some reason she felt betrayed. More so regarding her lack of knowledge and ignorance at how a person could have a completely different soul, a soul that never reflected in his outward being. She still believed in Sameer. She still had faith in his love for her and perhaps he no longer was the person he was years back when she had not met him. But the little details about Sameer she had picked up from his diary made her uncomfortable and slowly ate away at her faith, opening up a sliver of doubt.

8

THE DAYS IN OFFICE NOW no longer spent on brooding on mindless heartache, I bolstered myself up, realizing it was high time to be a man. I understood that there was no point in chasing false dreams. Dad's words, his expectations, and how I completed his world came back to me and the more I thought of the future, the clearer my goal became to me. What exactly would I gain by running behind futile things? It was time to let go and start life anew and with full vigour.

Those days, I did not end up going anywhere. Neither in a search for love nor for the search of a helping hand to support me and raise my sinking heart. I became almost indifferent to all pains and despair. My only motive was to clear the MBA entrance. After a month I went and joined an institute that would give me a better overview of things that I needed to look after in order to clear my CAT. There I met a number of other aspirants. Looking at them and their lives, I was not only inspired, their very presence in my life made me feel that I had just done the right thing by quitting meaninglessly chasing after girls. My days and nights were equal. I stopped calling anyone to ask for help. One day, Gaurav called me up. He was worried that I may have done something to myself.

'Hey man, where have you been?' he snapped. 'I was thinking about you, and getting a bit worked up.'

'I'm just fine, Gaurav. There is nothing to be worried about,' I tried to sound relaxed.

'See Sameer, I know you well. We have known each other for a very long time now. You mustn't be stressed about things which you have no control over.' He carried on, 'But you must understand that you have full control on what you can make happen. I would still hold by my words, that the cards do not say anything concrete. The future is only a reflection of your present.'

'That's exactly what I'm trying to do, Gaurav. I fooled around a lot. Now, I know my goals perfectly. It is the MBA and nothing else …'

He interrupted me suddenly. He took great joy in this habit of interruption but I always found the interruptions to be thought-provoking.

'Tell me one thing, have you heard of the story where Rama tried to hit the target with his arrow and ended up failing every time until Shiva whispered something in his ear?'

'No, actually,' I sighed.

'Ram once tried to hit the target with his arrow. But each time he focused on the arrow, he failed to have it hit the given dot. He grew frustrated and was wondering that even after having tried so hard, what exactly was the reason he couldn't. Just when he was contemplating, Shiva appeared. He said something in his ears and this time Ram could make his shot in one single go. Do you know what he said?'

'Mhhmm.'

'Think that the arrow has already hit the target. You only need to see it happening. Think that you have cleared it and you are already in your dream seat. You only need to see the course of the future changing in front of your eyes.'

I suddenly felt enlightened. I thanked him.

'Thanks so much, Gaurav! I know exactly what I need to do now.'

He smiled and asked me to let him know once I cleared the CAT. Such was his belief in me.

Next month, I went and gave the exam. As Gaurav said, I kept on reminding myself that this exam was only a projection of the fact that I have already cleared it. In the course of events, I had not only cleared it but was sitting where I wanted. I prepared nine papers and sent them to the best economics journals worldwide, I played my heart out and made good friends, if not on the personal front, at least on the professional front. I was almost compulsive with the idea of performance and nothing else could creep into my mind and heart. Love was at bay for those two years. Time ran its mill faster than my eyes and ears could perceive. The world, for me, was a giant block of numbers and determinants. I needed to be the best and that was all I knew. I did not even realize how the two years went by and how I found myself sitting for an interview for one of ATC's best jobs.

I called up Dad to tell him about the placements. But I had been carried away with a surge of emotion. I did want to tell Dad but it skipped me. His hopes for my success and his words were heavy in my heart. I felt elated and all my heartache washed away. I wanted to see his face when I gave him the news. I had to tell him that I had been placed in the company and that my office location was decided. I had been going there now and my first salary was due in a few days. I decided to call up home, assuming that these days Dad must be at home. He did say he would be, the other day.

'Hello.' My mother answered after five rings.

I remained silent.

'Hello, hello,' she continued to speak.

I tried to disconnect, but I heard her faint voice questioning me despairingly. For a moment I trembled, willing myself to say a word, but then thought the better of it.

'Why don't you talk to me? What I have done to you? You never talk to me.'

I could hold it no longer and disconnected the phone.

I waited for a few more minutes and dialled back again. After two rings, she again picked up the phone.

As I heard her voice, I chose to remain silent again. Without waiting, I wanted to disconnect the call again. I was getting irritated and thought of calling Dad on his cell phone. But just then she said, 'Wait, your dad is here. Talk to him.'

'Hello.' It was Dad.

'Hello,' I said.

'Why don't you talk to your mom? Now you are grown up. Does such kind of behaviour suit you, beta? So you won't talk to her. What happened between two of you again?' he said a reprimanding tone.

I interrupted him. 'Dad, I don't want to get into this. We have already discussed this several times. I have called to inform you that I have been placed. I had forgotten that day to tell you about my office but it's been quite some time since I joined and my first salary is due next week,' I said excitedly, ignoring the other things.

'That's really very good. How come you forgot to inform me the other day? By the way, which company was it? You said you were called by ATC, isn't it so?'

'Yes, yes. ATC. It's a good company. The package they have offered is also very decent.'

'Oh. That's nice.'

'Yes. By the way, my convocation is mid next month. I would like you to come this time. You couldn't make while I was in my engineering days. In fact, I too didn't attend the convocation. So this time, when everything is alright, please come.'

'Hmm. I will have to check if I can get leave. The elections are round the corner. So they have become quite strict. But still, I will try my best. If I come, I would like to bring your mom as well. Should I?' he asked.

'I don't want to hear any excuse. This work, that work. I also know how the government works. You have to come,' I protested.

'Should I bring your mom as well?' he again asked the question that I avoided purposefully.

'I don't know. It's up to you.'

'I have a better idea. Why don't you give this news to her yourself?'

'Because I don't want to.'

'She will feel good if you tell her personally. Also, invite her for the convocation. I am giving the phone to her.'

'No. I don't want to do anything. You can tell her this news.' But I didn't hear any sound. Probably he had already given the phone to her.

'Why can't you tell me? I am not your enemy?' She had heard me.

'Nothing.' And I disconnected the phone.

These kinds of small conflicts kept on occurring and I avoided them as much as possible. My not wanting to speak with Mom wasn't out of malice but was my way of running away from the situation. It took me to the time when things became ugly but I had, by now, left it to time to heal everything. Things that are to be improved will improve by themselves. I already had a lot of other things to think about and this could definitely be tackled later.

Just after completing my MBA, I decided to go home for two months. The placements were set and the company had given me the offer letter. I was due to join in July. They had not informed me of the exact date but I had calculated that it would perhaps be mid-July. By then I had known that I would be working in the Delhi office. I was elated and thought of a short vacation at home. I didn't know when I would get time to come next. I had also not seen Dad for quite some time.

It was noon when I finally reached the railway station with my luggage—two trolley bags and one shoulder bag. It was hectic shifting base. And I never liked it. The problem was that that I always had two to three extra bags. Every time I went somewhere I ended up carrying more and more bags. It was because I carried all my books and every month more and more books were added to the existing pile. I loved reading and books were my only respite. That night journey back home, however, did not give me any respite. It, in fact, turned out to be disastrous. Hoping to bump into some good-looking chicks, I had booked second-AC tickets. My fate had usually brought plump, crying babies onto my lap and all around me, and their bulging mothers, falling apart like cheese. This time I hoped for a change but no, my luck was not meant to be written in the heavens. All I could see around were children of various ages, babies crying louder than banshees, splitting my ears and bones. There was an aunty-ji in her fifties in the name of females. But I could hear giggles and roars of laughter coming from another compartment. Damn it! Why did this happen to me every time? My ill-gotten luck had backfired once again and I couldn't sleep the entire night.

Dad wasn't in town. He had already left for a remote place in another part of the state because of his office work. I could never understand his work profile and what exactly he did. Whenever someone asked me what Dad's profession was, I replied briefly that he was a state government employee.

So I had to come alone from the station. I got into the auto after arguing about the payment with the driver for several minutes. The sun was high up in the sky and dust from some construction work nearby engulfed our house.

I rang the doorbell. To my surprise, no one answered the door. I waited for a few moments and tried to hear if there were footsteps from the other side. Noting that there was no sound, I rang the bell again. There was still no response from the other side. I looked at the latch. It wasn't locked from outside. I tried to check whether it was open or not but it was locked from the inside. I was baffled, and grew impatient and tense.

I called Dad.

'Hello.' There was a lot of noise in the background.

'Hello. Have you reached home?' he shouted over the phone.

'Yes. But no one is opening the door. Is everything fine?' I said.

'Why? Mom isn't there or what?'

'I don't know where she is. I have rung the doorbell so many times and knocked at the door. Where is she?'

'Where could she have gone? She was there when I left home early this morning and locked the door behind me.'

'I don't understand what's happening. She is not responding. Should I try breaking down the door?'

'No. Come on. Maybe she is sleeping.'

'Maybe.'

'Do this. Climb up onto the roof and check from the kitchen side. Possibly she would hear you and wake up.'

I could sense worry in his voice now. But he hoped I would find a way.

'Okay, I'll do it. If there is still no response, I will break down the door.'

'Okay.'

I hurriedly disconnected the phone and ran towards the roof. I shouted several times from the kitchen side but there was no response. The whole neighbourhood had come to see what was happening. Ignoring them, I rushed back to the door and decided to break it.

Before breaking it, I tried again. 'Mom! Mom!' but nobody answered it. It was after a long time that I was saying 'Mom'. It felt unusual but I didn't it pay much attention.

I finally broke the door, and entered the house, calling, 'Mom, Mom.' No one answered. Sunlight filled the entire room. The temperature had risen dramatically. She wasn't in the living room. The fan was still on. The TV was also switched on and the daily soaps were going on at full volume. It meant she must have been here in the last few hours. I checked everywhere but there was no sign of her. I was bewildered.

The house was in a complete mess. There was a heap of trash on the kitchen floor. I shouted again, 'Mom' but there was, predictably, no answer. There was a deathly silence in the house. There was spilt milk on the kitchen slab and the gas was still on. The utensils had become coal black and smelled of burning milk. I turned off the gas and, as I did so, heard a faint sound from the balcony. I went towards it and saw her lying unconscious there, a bundle of dirty clothes clutched tightly in her hands. I rushed towards her and shouted again, 'Mom.'

I looked closely at her face. Her eyes were closed but looking at her, it appeared that she was struggling with all her might. Her lips were parted. I couldn't figure out what had happened.

'Mom,' I said gently.

She didn't open her eyes.

'Mom, Mom.' I tried to shake her. I knelt in front of her but she still didn't open her eyes.

Without wasting any more time, I called Dad. He was extremely worried and said that he was leaving for home in the next hour. I also informed my brother and he said that he would come try and come as soon as he could, if not today then hopefully by tomorrow.

My mind wasn't working at all. I was worried and concerned about Mom. Looking at her gentle face, I forgot all the bitterness of our relationship. Whatever it was, she was my mother. I cradled her tortured face on my lap.

She still hadn't opened her eyes. I was in a tizzy. What should I do? Should I call the ambulance? Should I move her into the house first and sprinkle water on her face? Had anything hideously wrong happened to her or was it just a hot flash because of the terrible sun, that she had lost consciousness? So many thoughts raced through my head but I only ended up gazing down at Mom. It took me back to the time when I was a kid and I was the one who was cradled. I was the one who looked up into her face and felt secure in the comfort of having her arms around me.

It had been several years that I had spent some good time with her. So it was difficult to see her face contorted. She was beautiful, my mother. I had spent several evenings with her telling me stories of how she had carried me from one house to the other while I was in her womb. Dad, back then, was struggling with his job and they had to change a number of houses because rents were going up. My brother was on the verge of completing his tenth grade and my mother had to look after him as well. It was a difficult period for her. Yet, back then, everything felt better when she told me that the joy of having a second child was even greater than the first and that, when she saw my face, all her pain and suffering left her. I felt all these memories coming back in a sharp daze, making me feel vulnerable.

'Mom,' I said. My heart pounded. But to my relief, she opened her eyes slowly and a smile spread across her face automatically, on seeing me. She appeared too weak to react to anything. She saw murmured my name and touched my face.

Her face was dull and pale, and her cheeks looked hollow. She was sick and I had kept myself away from her. I felt a deep pang of guilt and cursed myself for not having asked her even once how she was and if she needed anything. In fact, I hadn't even talked to her, fretting over silly familial disputes. I shouldn't have abandoned my mother like this. She seemed to have been sick a long time. She must have been suffering and no one was there to take care of her. She had tried countless times to reach out to me. She had almost pleaded with me to talk to her. It was I who had turned a deaf ear to her and her love. I could never understand her. The only thing I did was to ignore her. I thought, what possibly could have happened if I had talked to her once? Maybe this situation wouldn't have ever come up in the first place. Why does a person breed bitterness inside just to make things worse? I was not the kind of person who would allow such darkness to fill up his heart, and that too against my mother. I had been seeking love, but when I couldn't reciprocate properly to my mother's love, how on earth would I find or, rather, understand love at all? I felt strangled with guilt and remorse. I felt a strange force tearing my heart into bits. I was in a cloud of regret and gloom and could no longer hold back my tears.

Her eyes used to sparkle with her children around her. We were the stars and moons of her universe. Being young, it was in her eyes that we found comfort and the same eyes grew wise and red when we tended to break a rule or commit some nuisance. I could imagine her smiling at me when I told her how I had managed to get a seat in engineering. She couldn't understand much, nor could she compliment me like Dad, but in her eyes I did see the hope and satisfaction that her son had done something good which was worth being proud of. Now I could see the same eyes sunken beneath greying wrinkles. Her lips were bloodless. Like dry stitches on a wound, they were chapped. I took her hand between my palms and rubbed it, as if trying to compensate for all my past lovelessness. I felt grown up at that moment, as if cradling a daughter and not my mother. My soul condensed and thickened, and I was unable to move. In the process of growing up from a boy to a man, I had forgotten that my parents too had grown old. I had assumed, and that too blindly, that she could never be the perfect mother. Maybe because I never let her understand me. I was always indifferent and didn't bother to explain how I felt. I had acted in ways which were more than just imperfect. But I had to act soon. This wasn't the right time to brood. I had called for an ambulance and waited for it to arrive.

The ambulance arrived. I rushed outside, carrying her in my arms. She had again closed her eyes, her breaths long and shallow. I sat beside her till we reached the hospital, murmuring empty nothings to her. I placed one hand on her forehead and with the other I covered my own mouth, to prevent my gasping sobs from turning into ugly howls. I felt helpless and a zillion thoughts raced through my mind—bad thoughts, crippling thoughts, thoughts that forced me back to the time before things went wrong and ugly, before everything became a huge mass of despair.

'I am not your enemy. Talk to me.' I remembered her words, when she couldn't respond to me all the way to the hospital. I silently prayed that she would become fine and then I would do every single thing that I had not done for her in so many years.

She was admitted into the hospital. The doctor took his time checking her and I grew impatient with every passing second. I paced up and down the corridors of the dimly lit hospital and was on the verge of losing my patience.

After some time, I saw him coming out of her ward. I stumbled towards him.

'Doctor, is everything fine?'

'Yes, everything is fine. I think she fell down because of the heat and weakness. I have given her an IV of glucose but we cannot at this time detect if there are any more anomalies, or if she has had multiple deficiencies over a long period. We will have to do some tests and only after looking at the reports will I be able to tell you what exactly is her condition and how would we should approach it.'

The nurse had taken Mom's blood sample and the report would be coming in an hour or two. I could do nothing except wait.

She opened her eyes after an hour and the doctor let me talk to her. She asked in a low voice, 'How many days will you be here?'

I knew why she had asked this. For the last four years, I had made brief trips home, only once staying for seven days.

'I will be here for two months. And will only go after I'm sure you are healthy.'

I chatted with her for a few minutes, and then assured her that I would come back after collecting the reports.

As I turned towards the door, she called out my name. I stopped and looked back at her. She raised her head and mumbled, 'I am not your enemy. Please talk to me always.'

Tears rolled down my cheeks. There was a tight knot within me. Before it could uncoil into a storm, I turned my face away and left the room.

All the reports were normal except for the blood test and iron test. The doctor raised his brows when he noted her iron and haemoglobin levels. He asked how come I hadn't noticed the symptoms and chided me for getting Mom to the hospital at such a late stage. I felt guilty for being careless though I hand't been living at home. Dad and Bhaiya too had been away, so nothing could have been done. My sister was too young to know anything. So, I chose to stay quiet in front of the doctor.

He gave me a prescription with a list of medicines and asked me to take good care of Mom. He also made a list of foods that she needed to eaten regularly to regain her strength and stressed on fruit. While leaving, he patted my back. He had sensed my anxiety and told me not to worry. She would be fine soon.

The next day, I took Mom back home. She was still weak. Dad and Bhaiya had both arrived. I narrated the whole incident to them and informed them about what the doctor had advised. Dad said me that he was proud of the sensible way in which I had acted. But they both had to leave that very day both and I had to take on the entire responsibility of the house as well as Mom. I wasn't worried. Maybe I wanted it. This was necessary for us to re-forge our bond.

As a child, I had toyed with the idea of being disowned by my mother. I didn't know if it was love, protection, or her sense of misunderstanding her own child. Or maybe I had misinterpreted her actions. Whenever I went to the neighbouring aunty's place to watch a serial or *Chitrahaar*, Mom not only rebuked me but also cribbed about me in public. 'Don't tell me, Sunita, all day he just plays around and does nothing and then sneaks off to your place to watch TV. Someday I'm going to peel his skin off. I don't have any hope left for him.' The entire neighbourhood was familiar with this harangue. I wondered who would say such things about her own son. While I was growing up, there were similar instances which filled me with bitterness against my mother. She always had something bad to say about me. But when I passed tenth grade with flying colours, she stopped. She did realize her mistake which, in fact, was a by-product of her own cultural upbringing. She didn't know much about encouragement or inspiration. In her view, only gaalis and mindless reprimands sufficed and would do the necessary. Later, when she turned soft and her attitude towards me began to change, I was the one who became cold and unapproachable. I could see her pine for me even when I left home for college, but I didn't feel anything for her. I avoided her calls and never wrote to her. The bitterness of past memories was now in full bloom, consuming me with its malice and arrogance. Even when Dad called, I made it clear that I would keep my communication limited to him and not bother with Mom. I became a stone and considered never going back to her or ever listening, until the worst happened. I was wracked with guilt. However, I was fortunate that I had caught hold of the dwindling thread between our hearts in time.

A month passed by. Things became calmer. Mom and I bonded and her health improved. She was cheerful once again, both in body and spirit. I felt relaxed and as if time had turned back its wheel and mended every single wound, though I did feel a pang of longing for the lost days.

Dad was back and was happy to see mom hale and hearty. He had come home for my cousin's wedding. He insisted on taking Mom along with him, now that she was fine; she had not been out of the house for a long time. That night, I had my dinner early and went to bed as I felt weak and spent, though I had not done anything tiring at home. But sleep eluded me. I felt the temperature rising and my skin burning. I was feverish and my head felt heavy.

I decided to call up a doctor friend of mine and he asked me if I had paracetamol at home. I had a tablet and my fever subsided over the next one hour. Yet, I still couldn't sleep. I was instead reminded of another such day three years back, when I had been suffering from a similar bout of fever. Slowly my mind drifted into the void of the night and faded into the past. How long would it haunt me?

It was during the days when I about to complete my MBA. The academic pressure had lightened and I was taken as an intern at Citadel Steel Plant. I had by then achieved several of my career plans and was on the verge of living a happy life. To add to my happiness, I had befriended a girl on Facebook who seemed to be enamoured of me.

I was contemplating the lonely nights that had passed without my noticing in all these years and concluded that there are some nights when the soul seems to wander infinitely, searching for places, people, and lost memories, and seeks a future out of a silent storm. Then there are these nocturnal sufferers who cannot help but lie awake awaiting the dawn. I awaited a dawn in my life too, for I knew that every night, even the darkest one, is followed by the dawn. Light is victorious over darkness, the only thing being that darkness lasts longer. And it did that night, as I lay wide awake like an insect on its back, writhing in the heat, within and without. The fever was unbearable. The smog of the city, the concrete parapets, the humid, stale air—all of it added to the noxious atmosphere. My body felt roasted. I gasped at intervals for some fresh air, craning my neck desperately towards the window but the air was still and heavy. How would I pass this night? I turned back, thinking that the power of imagination is perhaps stronger than memory. For you believe what you want to believe and remember most what you would have given up, forgetting. Otherwise why do most people not like to talk or at times think of their past? There was nothing to do! I put my palm on my forehead and tried to gauge the temperature. How on earth would I feel anything? So let us imagine that since I didn't feel anything, I was perhaps troubled by something else and not fever. The weather, I suppose. The festive season, maybe. Everyone, including my roommate, had left for Holi. The morning would be full of colour. There would be happy faces marked with red, blue, and green. And I, wrapped in my sombre yellow bed sheet, would lurk around, trying to avoid phone calls from my parents and siblings. I had failed to get a ticket for home that year. A colourless year, rather. There was no excuse left to give either. What would I tell them? Should I complain about the ever-growing population of India proliferating like a tumour or should I tell them that such festivals were just useless in a country where people die like ants on the street? The fever was trying to get inside my imagination now, trying to force itself inside as memory does and make me believe that it was rising. I had no other tool to fight it except imagination itself. But heat makes the mind act like a thermos flask. It traps the mind and makes it vaporous and unclear. I got up fighting that aching realization and sat up like the Buddha, wrapping that bed sheet all around my body. The roof was the tree and heat compensated for the sun overhead. I opened my laptop and started browsing through Facebook. A usual, mundane activity. Bored more than ever, I flipped to the page where they post funny pictures, making a joke out of almost everything, and laughed to myself. I laughed to smash the fever out of my body. I laughed for it was the only medicine at hand with me now, but I wasn't successful. Suddenly, I saw a message blinking in my chat box. It was from her. She would often leave a small, brief message asking when I'd be free to talk. Like all memories registering faintly in the periphery of fame, I had remembered her words of praise but failed to remember her many messages. She might have sensed it then itself, so this time when she pinged me her only query was: Do you remember what I had written to you last? I told her what I remembered. Actually, I was confused. She was quiet for a while and then asked how I was. I just typed F-E-V-E-R. The brief, anxious letters spurted like bees out of a hive. She started enquiring about my food habits, lifestyle, what I had eaten last, if I had had too much junk food. I was surprised at the concern she showed. I whispered to myself, Is she a doc or what? I rushed to click on her blinking icon. Yes, she was a medical student. By the time I returned to my chat box, she had concluded all her advice on what medicine to take and what to eat, what not to as well. She was caring and I felt very good with her benign affection towards me. I couldn't say anything except, 'Thanks. So sweet of you'. I then asked her a few questions about herself and she started telling me several things as if we were old, close friends meeting after many years. I started thinking that this was fortuitous as the chat continued and felt relieved after chatting with her for nearly fifteen minutes. But I then had to stop as I started feeling uncomfortable with the fever. When I shut down the laptop, a faint, wistful smile lightened my brooding mind and her chat and care soothed my burning body. The night would pass.

Next morning, I woke up to shimmering sunlight. The fever didn't seem to affect me as much anymore. And my mind was quite clear. After drawing in the dust on the glass of my window, I checked my mail. Nothing. And as usual, I checked for any messages left on Facebook, even before I dragged myself to the pharmacy! There was indeed a message for me, 'Good morning. How are you feeling now? Let me know if you have taken the tablets. Be well. Shall be waiting to hear from you.' It was from her. And my smile was back. I had been wondering how to pass the cruel night and here it was, this dawn, awaiting me with a new light, lifting me through the rain. I had a hope for a hand to hold.

During the days that passed, we chatted continuously over Facebok. Her name was Tanvi. From the virtual world we graduated to talking over the phone, sharing everything that we could share—our aspirations, choices, desires, and many other things that made us fond of each other. I started feeling as if I had found a soulmate in her and was content to have someone beside me, though she was far.

She would often call me, 'Sameer, I hope I'm not bothering you ...'That would always be her first sentence. I would smile and tell her that she could neither bother nor disturb me, that I always waited for her call.

She gave me the belief that I was someone special to her. There wasn't an iota of doubt that she had opened up her heart to me and let me be its sole carrier.

'You know, it has become more and more difficult for me,' she'd mock the situation.

'Why? What's difficult now?'

'Well, you know I come back from the ward and attend to the clinic, read my books and then, in the middle of it all, I realize that the day has been a sheer waste. I have missed something important!'

'And what exactly might that be?' I would know the answer somewhere in my heart, yet I would not let on that I did.

'You know it, right? I know you're smiling. You dodo, it's talking to you over the phone.'

And we would laugh delightedly, continuing to talk for hours.

We would share the best and the worst of her life. She would share her petty problems at college and how she had to work long hours at the clinic. She would go on about how she longed to see me. She would tell me about her friends and how they all loved her. At times I felt she had too many people in her life and wondered if I was just the right one to be special among all of them. But we never ended up being serious on that matter.

After about two months, when my internship days were ending, she had her semester exams coming up. I refrained from calling her during those days as I wanted her to study well. I had it my mind that I would visit her once I was done with my MBA, of which I had barely some months left now. After her exams were over, called her. But, as time passed, I found her response colder and her spirit dwindling. Like all other tricks of fate, she too became distant and flimsy. All she talked about was her classmate whom she had started liking and the possibility of their becoming good friends in the future. I did not know how she could convert every single intimate detail into an area of common discussion. I still listened to her and consoled myself with the thought that she must be in a different mood altogether. Days crawled by with fewer and fewer words from her.

It was a month since I had finished my MBA. On the last

month after my exams I decided to visit her. I planned on taking the first train to her college and thought that I would surprise her. Maybe on seeing me, the dying embers of her heart would flare up. Maybe once she saw me, everything would come back to her and she would once again realize that I was the person she loved. Maybe on seeing me, every unsure feeling in her would turn into a certainty and we would end up together. But fate had other plans.

She called me up just the day before I had to take my train.

'Sameer, I need to tell you something.'

'What is it, Tanvi?' I had assumed that even before I reached there that she would tell me what I had longed for so many days.

'I think I have found my soulmate.'

'Me too …' I blurted out.

'Whoa! Really? It's Rishabh, actually. The classmate I had been telling you about. Remember?'

Her words struck me like an electric current and shattered every little piece of my world. I felt my knees crashing to the ground and the phone just slipped from my hands. For some time I couldn't quite gulp down my shock. But then I held my legs and squatted on the floor. I felt weak and unable to move. I had never thought of her as a frivolous person while talking to her about my life and how I was in need of love. Then she had said nothing and had acquiesced to being with me forever. But I didn't realize the change in her in a couple of months and that our bonding had become so mechanical. I felt broken, and more than that, I felt used. She, of course, knew of my feelings. Someone cannot be that ignorant as to not be able to detect the emotions in the voice of a person with whom she talked for hours, almost every day. If this was what she had in store for me, she either should have told me or should have never let me come so close to her so that I would lose myself. I wondered at the irony of this for days. Wondered at the incredulousness of people and how they could use others. Wherever I went, whatever I did, I found no peace. After having spent myself completely, I couldn't take it any longer. Instead, I decided to write a letter to her.

Dear Tanvi,

I am writing this to you with a heart that is weak with indifference. Within the last many months, seeing how close we had become, I had come to assume, and now too think, I know incorrectly, that you are the perfect person for me. You are perhaps the soulmate I was seeking since I was aware of something called love. But now I think this is causing me more harm than good. You have left me alone and vulnerable. You knew my feelings quite clearly as we had discussed them almost every day, that how desperate I was for love and my quest for love never seemed to end. Probably you are right in your own way, that you could not treat my feelings with greater perception than regular friends do. But in that process I was damaged somewhere inside. I became dark and unrecognizable, which I can no longer bear. It is definitely true that I need love and I pine for it, but that I cannot get it at the cost of chasing someone eternally and running after her without any hope. In the last few days I have observed your ignorance as well as your drifting away from me. I want both of us to be honest with each other and not make things ugly. You are surely lucky that you have loving friends to take care of you, the ones you have spoken to me about over the phone. I am happy that you have a life, unlike mine, where people are fond of you and want you in their life more than anything. But I cannot be a part of such a world. I want you as someone special, my special person, my beloved, and sharing you with others is naturally difficult. I have worked really hard to win people's hearts and that, with more of failure than success. Sometimes I feel terribly lonely and miserable for being what I am. What if I remain alone till I grow old and perish? What if I die alone without anyone beside me to talk to me during my last hours? But then, I would not have compromised on winning love on the grounds of losing my self-respect and self-esteem. More so, force doesn't work in a relationship. If it has to happen it will happen by itself. One cannot make it happen. For you, it must be easy to say that I was one of your good friends. But in my mind you had already completed and complemented me. I was already under the impression that we had given ourselves to each other. What, after all, is love if not giving? Perhaps that was a lie that I had been telling myself over all these months to keep myself from the reality but who can avoid reality? I was stupid. I have nothing much to say now. I feel broken. The thing that I wish for is to love and to be loved. I did my part honestly but you didn't reciprocate in kind.

The only strength I have at this moment is to understand my own aching self and let the world be ignorant about it. And now what else can I wish for you? You already have ample love in your life. And that too from your 'friend'. I did hope once that you would be the only person who would come forward and hold my hand. However, as they say, one must not lose hope. Maybe I will someday find someone who will love me for who I am, beyond friendship.

Best,
Sameer

Shagun kept the diary down on the table in front of her and looked up. The light of the day had slowly faded. In the afterglow of a heavy day she couldn't keep track of the wheel of time. Several hours had passed and it would soon be night. Sameer must have landed by now, she thought. He could call anytime. Thinking of him, she was filled with compassion. She thought it to be the wrong sort of feeling. For you feel compassionate for someone whose pain you think is of unbearable endurance. She was expected to long for him, not feel pity for him. But she couldn't feel that for the moment. She thought if she could have Sameer in front of her, she would cradle him like a child in her arms, kiss his forehead, and let him have what he had been seeking for so long—unconditional love. She needed to love him. She wanted to feel it desperately now. But for that she needed to finish reading the diary.

III

9

I WAS FEELING THE LOAD of years passing on my shoulders. Many of my friends already had full lives with wives and children. I had nothing of the sort to look forward to. People had drifted apart and were busy in their lives. Their time was for their family and not wasted, brooding, lonely, and desperate, like mine. I had no idea how they were and whether they were really happy to have a 'complete' life in the most conventional sense of the word. But their Facebook photographs did exemplify moments of euphoric happiness that is fabled to be found only with the existence of one's family. One of those days, Gaurav called up to ask me if I was well and how long I planned to brood.

'What do you need? You have the best life possible. Why do you have to make love, of all things, your ultimate obsession?' he snapped.

'Gaurav, you know it doesn't leave me, man,' I said, nodding like a school kid listening to his furious teacher.

'It slowly eats me up from inside and I have a feeling that this phase will never end, however successful I may become.'

'Precisely,' he interrupted me. 'Years have passed. You have managed to get through the best college and best job possible and people look up to you, you know, and you still haven't matured, Sameer. Do you think you are still a teenager or a college-going lover? Don't you think it's disappointing for me to know that you never believed in my predictions?'

'Gaurav,' I said, 'your predictions are the single silver lining in my dark sky.'

'Ah, come on,' he interrupted me again. 'Don't give me this melodramatic crap. Listen, I told you that the moment six bloody years of loneliness would get over you'll have your soulmate. That's the problem with you guys, you see: when I told you about cracking the best college and becoming successful, you did not consider that. Now, when you have the best job in hand, you don't appreciate my words of truth. Hmph!'

'Gaurav, that's not the case, you know,' I defended myself. 'Even after all these years, when I have lost contact with many of my friends due to their becoming settled with their wives and children, it's only you with whom I have maintained my friendship and I know you have always helped me to climb out of the rut of life.'

'Then you must also believe,' he said, his voice calmer, 'in the story I had told you once of Rama and Shiva. You are already with your soulmate. You just need her to find you and make you fall in love with her.'

And he hung up. His abrupt phone calls always lightened my burden. Though I couldn't really understand how the universe worked according to him, there was something about him that I couldn't help but believe in, each time that he said something and claimed it would turn true. Things would happen when they were meant to happen, as he had said. My convocation was coming up and I needed to prepare myself. I waited for the week to end.

Mom and Dad came for my convocation. That morning, I got up and took out my suit from the wardrobe. I did feel a bit vain but all my hard work was for Mom and Dad. The dean called me up on stage to deliver a speech on how I had managed to prepare nine papers and get them published in a span of two years, and I felt a surge of pride. The whole world shrank to the faces of my mother and father. I could see Mom's face brimming with joy as I was being praised in a crowd of over five hundred people. She didn't understand what I was being praised for, but she had the clear idea that her son had done something commendable and the laurels that followed made her feel that she herself had done something great. For me, it was certainly a cold war I had fought for years and not just to achieve what I did, but to slay the demons that had slept inside me. For the first time I felt I had won the world.

That evening Mom sat beside me and stroked my head which was on her lap. I pleaded with Dad to let her stay. After much insistence, he agreed. I was alone here and would feel better if she would stay with me for a while. Days passed and work became more and more hectic. I had been assigned with another responsibility at office. I was happy with this new responsibility because it was the best way for me to pass the time, without returning to my recent past that always led me into deep contemplation which got me to dig out things that disturbed me, and then resulted in sleepless nights. Mom was aware of these things, and that was the reason why she occasionally invaded my room at midnight, to check if I was asleep or not. Most times, she found me either sitting idly on the balcony, or working on the laptop. She would gently chide me, 'Beta, go to bed. It's already midnight. What are you doing so late in front of the laptop? I never understand.' And I would reply, 'Some office work, Mom.' She understood everything but never advised me. Because I never wanted to listen to anything. She knew it and did not want to stretch the matter lest it became ugly once again. Though sometimes she urged me to open up. I felt relieved that I had my mother to talk to, though I couldn't disclose everything about my heart's volatile condition to her. Dad spent his time between his office in Bihar and Delhi. He would come and stay with us most weekends.

One such evening, when I got home, I saw many plates

on the table and leftover namkeen, sweets, biscuits, and half-finished cups of tea. It must be a group of ladies, I thought. Mom had made good friends in the colony and there were aunty-jis moving in and out of our house since she came. It felt good. At least the house wasn't empty like before.

I sat on the sofa and picked up a sweet from a plate. I never understood how people could leave something like sweets untouched. I would never do that. First I would finish the entire plate and only then would I continue talking. Regardless of who was addressing me.

I loosened my tie and shouted, 'Mom! Where are you? I am back.'

She was in the kitchen and hurriedly came to the room. Her face was beaming. I wondered if Dad had gifted her a necklace or some new sarees. But I asked her directly, 'You're looking very happy. What's up? By the way, so many plates ...' Before I could finish, she interrupted me as if she just been waiting for an opening, 'Seema Aunty had come.'

I raised my eyebrows and said, 'Who is this Seema Aunty?'

'What? Don't you remember her? You met her at Aanchal Aunty's anniversary party? Last to last week.'

'Mom, how could I remember anyone? In the last two weeks, we have been to at least five parties. And I never understand why you insist on taking me along to such parties,' I said jocularly.

'Yes beta, I understand. But you remember one aunty who remarked after meeting you that you looked very handsome in your blue sherwani,' she tried hard to remind me.

'Yes, yes. I think now I'm able to recollect faintly. It didn't appear that it was her fortieth anniversary. I must say, she has maintained herself quite well.'

I waited for Mom to say something but she remained silent. When I looked at her, she protested, 'Why? Does your mom look like an old hag? So many ladies in the party mentioned, that too several times, that it doesn't at all appear that I am the mother of three and that I'm over fifty-five. Huh.'

'Mom, Mom!' I cajoled her. 'You are the most beautiful lady on earth. Happy now?' I said, with a big smile on my face.

'Yes. That's better. So at that time, Seema Aunty was also there, she had asked you about your job and all.'

'If you say so. Even if I beat my head against the wall I'm not going to remember anything, Mom. And who cares about aunties in parties!' I chuckled. 'I attend parties only to eat. If you ask me, I can easily remember the names of the various delicacies we had that evening.' I laughed.

She laughed too. I felt good to see her laughing.

'So what about Seema Aunty?'

'Yes. She was saying that Rekha, your son has grown up. He's a naujawan now! Aren't you thinking of his shaadi?'

'So …' I didn't like where the conversation seemed to be going.

'So, she was saying that she has a girl in mind. Very beautiful …' I stopped her.

'Mom, why are these aunties always so worried about my marriage, tell me?'

'Oh. Listen to me na, beta. Kabhi toh sun!' she snapped. 'I too want you to get married. You will be thirty-one soon. And I also want a bahu who will take care of me.'

'Then it's fine. I will arrange a nurse for you who will take care of you all the time. Moreover, you both won't even fight. In fact, you can make her do whatever you want without her uttering a single word. Wouldn't that be nice?'

'No, I want a bahu. And that's my final decision.'

'Okay, okay. But you always go on about a beautiful girl. The last dozen girls were also beautiful. And you know what happened with them. So, sorry. I am not going to meet this new girl.'

'First listen to me. At least get to know her. See her photo. Read her biodata. And then decide.'

'No, Mom!'

'Listen. Either you bring home a girl of your own choice or let me decide on a suitable lass for you. Here, Seema Aunty has given me a picture of her. First you see her, and then decide. I won't say anything.' And she went into the other room.

When lines like 'I won't say anything' come up, there is

seriously no option but to listen to Mom. She's a typical Bollywood mom, I swear.

She came back with an envelope in her hand. Looking at her beaming face, I was sure that she was hell bent on settling this girl and me together. She put the envelope into my hands and said, 'Open it up and see.'

'Don't I have any option other than opening it?' I sighed, making a face.

'Don't say anything and open it,' she ordered.

I took out the picture and looked at it. I looked at the picture then at Mom. I thought Seema Aunty had perhaps given her the wrong picture. And then I looked at Mom again.

She asked, 'What happened?'

'Are you sure this is the picture of the girl?' I asked, bewildered.

'Yes. That's what she has given me. Why?'

'Because there are so many girls dancing. How on earth could it be the picture of a girl sent to a prospective groom to look at?' I mocked. 'Where is that picture of the girl by the flowerpot wearing a constipated smile?' I laughed loudly.

'Actually, Seema Aunty has only this picture of her. She asked me to keep it for now. By tomorrow she will ask Kajal's parents personally. She is going to their place.'

'Oh! Kajal is her name, whoever she is in the picture,' I said and then protested, 'Wait, what do you mean that she will go and meet her parents? Don't tell me that she is distributing pictures of a girl without her parents' knowledge. Isn't that absurd?'

'You are another one. Why do you have to analyse everything? This is women's stuff. You just tell me whether you liked the girl or not. Rest we will see. Isn't she beautiful?' she beamed.

'Beautiful? First tell me, where is she in this picture?'

'Oh. That's her in the left corner. She was clicked while dancing.' She looked at my frowning face. 'And yes, that answers your question—she is a dancer.'

'Don't worry. Bring in a dancer bahu and she will make you dance all day,' I quipped.

'Be serious sometimes. You always have to make fun of things.'

'Okay, okay. I am serious. Let me check out this girl.'

I tried hard to find the girl. But there were four girls dancing in the corner.

'Mom, sorry, but I don't know who is your bahu Kajal. Here four girls are dancing in the left corner.'

'Okay.' And she pointed straight without taking a second. I looked at the picture closely. She was in a typical red suit, the kind of red people wear only for their wedding. I have a great aversion for these red-suit kinds. In fact, all the other girls were wearing the same flashy red. I could not see the girl properly. She had her head hung forward and her hair was loose around her face. It appeared for a moment that she was doing the salsa.

'Is she doing the salsa?' I asked Mom, trying hard to see what exactly this girl was doing.

'What … sa …? She is doing bhagnra.'

'Never mind.'

'Okay. How is she?'

'Mom, did she drink bhang and dance the bhangra?' I asked.

'Why are you saying so?'

'Because I am not even able to see her face. Look at the picture. All her hair is on her face. It seems like she is doing an ad shoot for some hair product.'

'Oh. Don't worry about that. Seema Aunty will bring another picture of hers. Tomorrow. But I feel you should meet her.'

'I have said it earlier as well. I don't want to meet anyone.'

'Only once. You didn't meet anyone,' Mom pleaded.

'Yes, because I don't want to meet any such bimbos. All stupid girls.'

'How can you say that without even meeting the girl? Meet her. Talk to her. Try to get to know her. I am not forcing you at all.'

'Okay, okay. I will see. By the way, what does the girl do except dance?'

'She cooks very well. Any kind of dish.'

'No, I am not asking this. Is she educated?' I corrected Mom.

'Yes.' Mom said as though she was the CEO of some company.

'She is some soft … umm … engineer. See, she is an engineer.'

'Okay. Software engineer. Where?'

'Yes. The same. Seema Aunty was saying that she works at some company named Info-fy-fush.' Mom tried to recall the name but found it hard to pronounce and so let it go.

'Okay. I got it. It's Infosys.'

'See? You also like her education background.' She beamed again.

'What? When did I say that?' I said, nonplussed at her interpretation.

'Okay. Done. I will fix a meeting with Seema Aunty.'

'Do whatever you like. I am very hungry. Call me whenever the dinner is ready. By the way, what is Dad up to?'

'He must be loitering around the sector, looking for some paan. After coming back home, nowadays he has developed a very bad habit of eating paan along with his new-found friends in the colony.'

'Nice. Don't bother him. He has worked hard throughout his life and has toiled enough.' As soon as I saw Mom making a face, I continued, 'You have also worked very hard. Everything will be fine. I am going to change things for us. Acha, now call me when dinner is ready.'

I went into the room and closed the door. After

freshening up, I changed into casual clothes and came out on the balcony.

It wasn't completely dark. The sun was slipping out of the sky and birds flew in a line, splitting the patch of sky overhead. I could see red fading to black. The breeze felt welcoming and soft. I decided to spend some time on the balcony till Mom called me.

I pulled out a chair and sat, resting my legs on the parapet, and was soon lost in a whirlpool of thoughts that led me to the past. It had been almost a year since the Tanvi fiasco. I still couldn't understand how things had turned out this way. I felt unwanted. Whatever reason I tried to give myself resulted in the thought that it shouldn't have happened this way. It was heartbreaking. Everything was set. I had even informed my parents but nothing favoured me. A few weeks back, I came to know that she had got married to the same guy, her classmate. I knew she must be happy with the love of her life but a question that always haunted me was when I would meet my love of my life. Or, rather, *if* I would ever meet the love of my life. Was there really someone who thought like me and believed in love the way I did? I knew it was difficult. My previous experiences made me doubtful but I had no choice but to wait. It was not a thing I could try and make happen. Love isn't an ambition that a man can pursue and achieve. While I was still pondering over these questions, Mom tapped me on my shoulder.

'I was looking for you in the room. In fact, Dad also called you but you didn't hear. So, I came to call you'

'It's okay, Mom! Why do you have to be so apologetic?' I said to her, looking at her sullen face.

She rubbed the back of my head.

'What are you thinking?' she asked.

'Ah, nothing. Just office work. They have assigned me some new responsibilities,' I lied.

'Don't lie to me. I know you are thinking about what happened.'

I didn't answer.

'You know your dad and I were ready to talk to her parents. Who knew this would happen. Everything is fate and destiny, beta.'

'No, it's all about my fate, that of unrequited love. What do I lack? I am good-looking, earn handsomely, I'm caring. What else does a girl need? But it always happens with me. I can't understand this.'

'Don't be upset, beta. Things happen for a reason. Probably you will find the reason very soon. It's all a matter of time.'

'Time? Huh. A decade has passed since I have been in a romantic relationship. People have made fun of my affection and honesty. I never cheated on anyone but nothing has ever been in my favour,' I vented my frustration.

'Don't worry,' she said as she stroked my hair. She knew that it always made me feel good. She pulled out a chair and sat beside me. 'Why don't you go and meet your friends? You will feel better.'

'I am not interested.' I knew if I went out, everyone would ask me when I was getting married. It had started to irk me. I didn't want to answer such questions. It always reminded me that I had been deprived of love. I was a man of unrequited love.

'You should go out,' Mom interrupted my reverie. 'You will feel better. I know everything will be fine. You have made everything better for us and you know what, you will get the best girl who will respect you and love you for what you are.' I could feel her reassurance in the way she smiled at me. Her belief gave me solace, if not strength.

'Okay.' I shrugged.

'Now don't get upset. Dinner is ready. Your dad is already at the dinner table, hogging! Let's go otherwise he will finish all the rotis, even without any gravy. I have made chicken for you.'

I smiled.

As per Mom's prediction, Dad already had started chewing on his roti without any gravy.

'What are you doing?' Mom snapped at him.

'Eating roti. Come son, sit here.'

'Can't you wait?' she scolded Dad.

'No. Don't listen to your mother,' Dad said to me, ignoring my mother, and put a plate in front of me.

Mom laid out the dishes on the table and we started eating.

'I will have two more rotis today,' Dad announced.

'Why? By the time you finished discussing how the world had gone to dumps and how the politics of this country is a sheer waste, with your so-called old mates, you weren't hungry at all. And now, what happened suddenly?' Mom commented.

'Yes. That was a one-hour-old story. Now you have cooked chicken. I know it's for your son but being your husband for the last many years, I can hope for two more pieces.' And we all laughed together.

'So how is your job going on?' Dad asked.

'It's fine,' I replied briefly.

After a few minutes of silence, I made up my mind and said cautiously, 'Dad, Mom, I was thinking for the last couple of days that I should go out somewhere. It has been a long time since I have gone anywhere. What do you say?'

'I have no problem at all.' Dad never said no to my decisions and wishes.

'I also just suggested to you to go out somewhere. Life becomes boring living in the same place for a long time. So where do you plan to go?' Mom asked.

'I am planning to go to Shimla. People say April is a good month to visit Shimla. So I guess I will be there for around two to three days.'

'It's fine. When are you thinking of going?' Dad asked.

'This weekend. I will apply for leave on Friday. So it will be a three-day weekend.'

'That's absolutely fine,' Dad said, munching on the chicken.

'Oh god!' Mom exclaimed.

'What happened?' I asked.

'Just look at your dad. He dropped gravy on his shirt again. I am tired of this man.'

'Where?' Dad asked casually as he looked at his shirt and wiped the gravy, which spread. Mom rushed into the kitchen to get a wet cloth.

I returned to my room after dinner and slid into bed. I allowed my mind to be trapped again in the web of my past to unravel the mystery that had been plaguing me for so long.

10

NEXT DAY, SEEMA AUNTY CAME with the picture, as promised. When I came back from office, Mom showed me the new photograph. Without arguing with Mom, though her face was beaming as if she had hit the jackpot, I didn't ask or say anything but took the picture out of the envelope.

As expected, she was standing beside a flowerpot. Typical rishta-type picture.

I looked at the photo. Of course she looked beautiful, though it was evident that she had on half a kilo of make-up.

'So … she is beautiful, isn't she? I told you yesterday also but you didn't believe me,' Mom said.

'Hmm. She is beautiful but I hope she has some brains too.'

'Yes. She has. I have met her. She is religious too and goes to the temple every Saturday unlike you who keep yourself miles away from the temple and call yourself a nastik.'

'Why Saturday only? God is happy with her all other days or the temple's priest has banned her from going there every day?'

'Nice. You keep making fun of everything. Just see your age. It is zooming on. When will you get married and when will you have children?'

The same melodrama was about to start again and I would have to do my best to avoid the shenanigans.

'Mom, I am going to change. Call me when dinner is ready.'

Ignoring me, she asked, 'Then shall I fix a meeting with them? I have to send a message to her parents. They are ladki-wale. So, they might have some arrangements to welcome us.'

'Whatever suits your fancy,' I said curtly, and went to my room.

Later, while at the dinner table, Mom informed that she had fixed the meeting and all of us would be going to meet the girl on Thursday evening. I would be leaving for Shimla the next day.

On Thursday morning, Mom said as I was leaving for office, 'Please be early today. You remember we have to go to their place.'

'Mom, you have already told me four times since the time I have woken up. I remember perfectly. Why don't you inscribe it on my forehead?' I said in a mocking tone.

And I left for office. She called me thrice even there

to remind me and messaged me five times. I cursed myself for teaching her how to send SMSes. Every time she called, I just replied that I remembered and would be home early.

I reached home around five in the evening. To my surprise, Mom was already ready, wearing her best saree, and had loaded herself with all the gold she possessed. Dad was also ready in his designer kurta and smiled at me as he opened the door. I knew it was Mom who had forced him to wear traditional attire.

'Beta, get ready soon. We are getting late.'

'Why the hurry, Mom? We have to get there by seven, right? It is still five.'

'Yes, but Seema Aunty is also coming with us. She will be here any minute.'

'Why is she is coming? In case I reject this girl, then would she try to set up her own son with her?'

Dad laughed. Mom gave Dad a glare that made his laughter vanish in a matter of seconds.

'No, she is coming with us because she knows the ladki-wale very well and she will be introducing them to us.

'Okay. Chill. Tell me what to wear,' I asked Mom.

'A kurta is fine, the kurta that I bought for you along with your father's. The one he is wearing now.'

I took around fifteen minutes to get ready, by which time Seema Aunty had arrived with her paraphernalia. The moment I came out, all three of them stood up as if they were waiting to accompany me to a war.

Herself draped in a heavy designer saree and more jewellery than Mom was wearing, it looked like it was her son's wedding! She also had a three-inch thick layer of make-up on her rotund face.

I greeted her. She smiled as if someone had smacked several gulab jamuns together in her mouth. Her redder-than-blood lipstick hid her teeth.

We left for Kajal's place. I wanted time to speed up so I could leave for Shimla and get a break from my routine life. After half an hour of driving, we reached their home. From outside it seemed to be simply built, but I was utterly mistaken. The interior was extremely polished and magnificent.

My mom winked at me. And as usual my father had no comment to make about the interior. Nor about me.

Kajal's mother was waiting for us. She too was dressed in the best of her attire, a big smile pasted on her face and her eyes beaming with zest. It was evident that she wanted to get her daughter married off before the sun went down. I went ahead and greeted her. She exchanged pleasantries with us and asked us to sit. The greetings continued for several minutes as she hugged Seema Aunty and then my mom. I was already getting bored. The table was heaped with delicacies—sweets and namkeen.

With a perfunctory smile, Seema Aunty said, 'Ah! What

was the need for all this? We've already had our evening snacks.'

'Oh, it's nothing much! How can you go from our house without having anything?' and she looked at my mom.

My mom smiled. She was happy. In between this stupid conversation, I didn't know what to do with myself. I sat quietly, staring at their jubilant faces and seething at my mom.

After a few minutes, when Kajal's mom saw that I had not touched the snacks, she asked, 'Beta, why are you not eating? Have some snacks?"

I smiled and said, 'Sure, Aunty.'

'Aunty? She might become your mother-in-law, son! Seema Aunty joked. And all of them started laughing as if they had cracked world's funniest joke. I suddenly became her son-in-law when I hadn't even seen her daughter. What silliness!

I started munching on the namkeen. I looked at my dad at the other end. He was busy eating and was indifferent to the hustling, animated conversation happening all around him. He was hogging on almost all the food items and was busy having his samosa, when Kajal's father came in. He greeted him with a piece of samosa in his hands. I greeted him too.

I noticed some girls frolicking in the other rooms and glanced at them. All of them looked more beautiful than Kajal. Swiss author and businessman Rofl Dobeli's statement was absolutely correct that when one has so many factors in front of one while choosing a girl, one ends up looking for physical attractiveness. That was perhaps the simplest way to pick up a girl. Because I was in no mood to select anyone where I overlooked this factor also. But one question still lingered in my mind. Why had so many girls come over to a prospective bride's place? I was ruminating on the question when Kajal's father interrupted my thoughts. He started asking me about my job and what I did on a day-to-day basis. They asked my salary and when I told them, the whole room suddenly went quiet and Kajal's parents looked at each other.

Mom said, 'We would like to meet Kajal now. What do you say?' She looked at Dad, who was busy cleaning the sauce he had spilled on his kurta.

'Yes, yes,' he managed to say, smiling meekly.

'Yes, sure, why not.' And Kajal's mom called for Shweta.

'Yes, Aunty?' She came running. She was stunning and looked like she was the bride.

She went off to summon Kajal. I just wanted to meet her, wrap up this drama, and leave the place. I was waiting for the next morning to leave for Shimla. I had never been so excited about going to a new place and travelling but this was probably the last hurdle to cross.

Kajal was taking some time. Seema Aunty, to lighten the moment and fill the silence, said, 'It seems she is getting ready. Girls take time to get ready and moreover this is a matter of marriage.'

So that she can cheat the groom's parents by covering herself in tons of make-up, hiding her real identity, I thought.

Kajal came slowly from the other end of the room along with a friend on either side supporting her as she carried in a tray. Then I saw that there was no teapot on the table. Only then did I realize that something had been missing from the table. It was all getting so filmi that my irritation knew no bounds. Why does everything that's got do with Indian marriage need to be so quintessentially pretentious? Why don't girls and boys meet and fix up a marriage like a contract and sign it, if at all arranged marriage was supposed to be an official association without prior knowledge of both the parties. It would have been simpler and people like me could be saved from such mindless drama.

Her friends helped her sit on the empty sofa seat before she kept the teapot on the table.

She greeted everyone and at last looked at me. I nodded slightly to acknowledge her greeting. She was in a blood-red sari with dots all over it. She was fair, with a good height. It was clear that she had on tons of make-up but the red mark that she had drawn between her eyebrows made her really beautiful.

Everyone turned towards her and started asking her questions. After a short interview, my mother beamed and looked at me to suggest that her quest to find a suitable girl for me had finally ended. She had the face of a winner. I always wanted to see this winning smile on her face but I knew this time I was going to disappoint her. It was not because Kajal was either a good or bad girl or suitable for me but the point is that I never wanted to marry someone who didn't know me properly because many a time my mom and dad themselves had difficulty in understanding me even though I had stayed with them for so many years. There were thousands of differences between us and it was difficult to address and solve all of them. I did not want that to happen with at least my partner. If at all there were differences, I wanted us to be able to come to the root of them. Which was only possible if she knew me. The idea of marrying someone and being bound to her for life without having known each other somehow did not fit into my system. Ever. In fact, it was horrifying to think of such a thing.

Mom knew that until I decided, there was no chance of finalizing the girl. So she was a bit apprehensive and gazed at me hopefully. I smiled at Kajal and soon everyone left us to talk in private. An HR interview! A technical interview was remaining to confirm if she knew how to cook, and so on.

I didn't know what to say and how to start. I had avoided such meetings many times in the past. Once when I decided to meet a girl, she didn't come as she wanted to marry her boyfriend. At that time, I just drank a cup of coffee alone and came back and told Mom that it was all fine but the girl wasn't ready and that she had explained her situation to me.

But soon Kajal solved my problem. And started the conversation.

'So you are a banker?'

'Yes,' I replied briefly.

'A money man. It must be an exciting job. Money all around. Hai na?'

'Umm. Initially it looks good otherwise it's not as exciting as it looks from the outside.'

'When you have money then what is left to think about, tell me.' Our conversation had started on the wrong note. Kajal seemed more interested in my money than in me.

'Probably true. So what you do? I mean, any job?'

'Not yet. Searching for a job, actually. My friends were saying there is a vacancy in a bank. You have an idea about banks. What do you think?'

'I haven't much idea. I am not with a commercial bank. I am in mergers and acquisitions. If your friends are saying so, it must be good.'

'Yeah, I too am thinking the same. So where should we go for our honeymoon?' she asked.

'Honeymoon? Sorry? We are not married.'

'Yes. But we will be. No? Don't you like me? I mean, look at me. I am beautiful, am I not?'

'Yes. You are.'

'Then what else do you need? You have a girlfriend?'

'Hmm. No.'

'Okay. Then your life must have been boring so far. Don't worry, once I marry you, I will make your life exciting. I am a fun-loving girl. So what's your favourite country?'

'Haven't thought about it. Probably New Zealand, I guess,' I said. I really had no idea where this conversation was heading. But I really New Zealand and kept it on the second position of my dream destinations after watching the *Lord of the Rings* movies.

'Oh, great. I love Paris.'

'Have you been there?'

'No, but Eiffel Tower is the most romantic place for me.'

'Good choice, I must say. Do you read?'

'Ah, that's boring. I tried reading a book once but kept it aside after a few pages, and returned it to my friend!' she exclaimed as if exhibiting a prize.

'Oh. Great.'

'Do you read?'

'Yes. Sometimes.'

'Means you are not interested in having girlfriends?'

'What makes you assume this?'

'Because people who read generally have a lot of time on their hands and they wouldn't want to spend or waste time with a girlfriend, doing all sorts of things.'

'Oh. Wow. By that logic, it must mean that you don't read because you have a boyfriend or boyfriends,' I said sarcastically.

She laughed. Probably she didn't notice my last words and continued, 'I had. Every beautiful girl has to have a boyfriend. It's a status symbol, you see.'

'Oh. Pity on me that I am last in the race.' I had reached my height of irritation now and wanted to leave the room as soon as possible. Perhaps this city, if I had to deal with such people on a daily basis. I wondered if I should gulp down my tea so that I could leave sooner. I didn't have any idea of how to stop this conversation. Think, Sameer. You give so many financial solutions to clients, you can surely think about this too, I encouraged myself but she blurted out another question that really shocked me.

'So what do you think?' she asked.

'About what?'

'You know very well why we are here. For our marriage. Aren't you? Or are you lost in some dreamy book?' She laughed. I didn't like that.

'Ah. I am not in any dream. Isn't it too soon? It's a matter of our lives, isn't it?'

'Yes. But you know what, you will find me cute and will be happy with me. My boyfriend said the same thing.'

'Oh. Then why don't you guys get married? It would be a better idea, actually.'

'I wanted to but his parents weren't ready as we are from different castes.'

'Okay,' I replied briefly so as to end this conversation.

'You didn't answer. I like you. You are shy. I like your mild mannerisms. Viraat is also like you.'

'Nice. I may need some time. Let's go to where everyone's sitting.'

We came out of the room. Our parents were waiting for us. Kajal was smiling and looking at her smile, Mom winked at me.

I must clear her confusion, I thought.

'So, how was it? Did you like Kajal?' her mother asked.

I was reluctant to say anything at this moment. I nodded and said, hesitantly, 'Yes. Everything had gone fine but since it is a lifetime decision, I may need some time.'

'Sure, beta. Take your time.'

11

'WHAT? BUT WHY?' MOM SHOUTED.

'I don't want to. You were not in the room.' I didn't want to extend this conversation.

'What happened? She is beautiful and cooks well. She prepared the snacks you were hogging.'

'If you want someone who cooks well, then hire a cook.' I knew this conversation wasn't going to end any time soon because the moment I would try to end it, Mom would start on another topic. It was the fifth time we were discussing Kajal.

'She's very good. And she is so beautiful too!' Mom protested.

'She doesn't even read books!' I declared.

'So what? I don't also read books. If I am illiterate then you wouldn't consider me your mother or what? You father doesn't know English well, so you wouldn't consider him your father? What stupid thinking is this? She doesn't read novels, huh,' she fumed.

'Mom,' I tried to cool her down and put my hand on her shoulder. 'It's not like that. I never said that I wouldn't get married. I will definitely marry someone who understands me. You know how tough it is to understand me, to get used to my eccentricities. It's not about you and Dad. It's about me. Marriage is a big responsibility. I want to be with someone who can understand us and can hold our home together. We have suffered enough. I can't marry this girl who kept talking about her boyfriend. She doesn't have any sense to understand you and Dad, how would she handle me? It's not about being beautiful. You can find thousands of beautiful girls out there. But it doesn't mean that all of them are perfect for marriage. I want a sensible, independent, working girl who has some sense, who can take care of you and Dad in my absence. What would be the point of getting married to a girl who doesn't know anything, for whom everything is just about fun? You know what her main question was?'

'What?' Mom had calmed down a bit.

'It's funny. She asked where we would be going for our honeymoon.'

'What is wrong with that question? When you get married, you will definitely go to some place for your honeymoon.'

'Mom. That's not the point. Who asks such question at

the very first meeting? Of course, Kajal can,' and I laughed.

'Son, see, you are already thirty. Who will marry if you are older? Twenty-seven to twenty-eight is the perfect age for marriage and you have already crossed it.'

'Don't worry. First of all, stop saying I am growing old. I am perfectly fine and don't look aged. And you will get the world's best daughter-in-law. Trust me,' I said, looking into her eyes. I continued, 'Okay, I have to go to Shimla tomorrow. So now I am going to sleep.'

'Wait, wait. You have to do one more task in Shimla apart from your sightseeing.'

'And what is that?'

She went into her bedroom and the next minute came back with a card in her hand. I was puzzled. Was it a shopping list? But the card was decorated.

'It's a marriage card,' she said. I waited for her to continue.

'It's your dad's friend's son wedding card. They are organizing everything in Shimla, a neutral venue. They have invited us but I told them that we wouldn't be able to come, but our son will be in Shimla on Friday and will attend on our behalf.'

'Why did you say so? Mom, you know very well that I am not going to Shimla for this. And you know how much I hate attending weddings and parties.'

'I know, son, but we can't avoid this invitation. He is a very close friend of your dad's and it would be just a matter of half an hour. Go, give the gift to the couple, eat, and come back. It's nothing much.'

'Okay, I will think about it.' And I took the card and went to sleep.

I left for Shimla in the early morning on Friday. I had already booked a cab the previous night and the driver was expected to reach around 7 am. But my journey began an hour later despite my being fully prepared and waiting for the cab. I had already double-checked the stuff in my bag, counted all the items, and re-checked against my list to ensure I hadn't missed any item.

Mom and Dad came to see me off at the gate. As soon as the cab arrived, I threw the bag inside and sat on the back seat. I had mixed feelings on finally going on vacation. I hadn't listened to Gaurav who had repeatedly suggested that I visit a new place and have fun. But I had ignored his advice, and now I wondered why. For the first few minutes, I wouldn't say I was too excited or even felt anything because of familiar surroundings. But eventually, as the cab kept moving and I left behind the surroundings I was accustomed to, I started feeling a bit excited.

The sky was cloudy and a cold wind awakened my senses. As we moved closer to the mountains, it started getting chillier and I had to put on my jacket. The earth looked green and new and there were masses of bushes lining the highway. I cursed myself for having delayed this trip for so long. I should have done this much earlier. The serpentine road snaked through the mist to steep gorges and valleys. I lowered my neck and stretched to see the other side of the valley I was going through, but the dense foliage covered my vision and trees lined the sides of the roads such that I couldn't see what lay beyond the mountains. I felt exhilarated and the splendour of the place swept me off my feet. I asked the driver to stop the car for a while. I got out of the car and inhaled deeply. Everything seemed new and welcoming. The fragrance of pine dust filled the air. The valleys sprawled, creases along it splitting its peaks and gorges. The trees rose up like tall, old women, their hair loosened in the wind. I moved ahead to get a better view but couldn't see anything. The driver saw me craning my neck and trying hard to see through the mist. He called out, 'Sir, if you want a better view, just walk ahead a little and you will be surprised at the lovely view.'

'Really? Or do you just want me to go away so that you can vanish?' I said.

'What are you saying, sir! I know about the view because so many tourists go to that point. They mostly stop here and walk a little bit. I have accompanied some of them,' he said excitedly.

He accompanied me to the point. It was, indeed, the most marvellous view that extended for miles and miles. I could see mountains in the distance and in between them land that rose and fell gently and was crowded with trees and hedges. It was an amazing feeling to stand at that point with the silence of the mountains all around me and a light breeze caressing my face. For a moment, I was rejuvenated and forgot about all my problems. I remained there for several minutes, breathing the fresh air and releasing all the negativity and sadness of my life. The chill air and the green exuberance made me shout in delight; I was surprised as it had been many years since I shouted because I was simply happy.

I was glad that I had come out of Delhi.

'Sir, for how many days will you be in Shimla?' the cab driver asked as we resumed our journey.

'Two to three days. I am not very sure about it right now. Why?' I replied, looking at him in the mirror.

'If you need a cab on the way back, please call me. I will also be returning to Delhi on Sunday evening,' he said, and gave me his phone number.

'Okay, sure. What's your name?' I wanted to continue this conversation. Feeling rejuvenated, I wanted to get to know something new. To know about a new person from a new place. Perhaps he could tell me about the best places to visit in Shimla.

'Sir, Vishu.'

'Oh. And you belong to?'

'Sir, I don't know.'

'What do you mean?'

'Sir, I was brought up in an orphanage. I learnt how

to drive near the orphanage itself. So I don't know which place I come and who my parents are.'

'Oh, I am sorry.' Sometimes we get so involved in our day-to-day problems that we forget there are many people out there who are less fortunate than us and are suffering deeper problems than ours. This helped me put my life in perspective. When I imagined a life without my parents, I felt scared and for a moment, almost forgot my problems. I understood that whenever one faces a problem, one should look at the people who have lived a harder life than one and who have worked harder than one to get what one already has by luck and inheritance. And that will make one forget all of one's problems.

'Sir, actually the orphanage I was raised in is near Shimla. So I know this place well. And coincidently, tomorrow it's the fiftieth anniversary of the orphanage. I always go there for the anniversary celebration no matter where I am. It was luck that this time I got a passenger for Shimla directly. So I will earn some money and buy sweets and clothes for the children in the orphanage because once I was one of them.' His voice took on a tender, sentimental tone.

It happens. I could easily understand him. It is far easier to say something that is very close to our hearts to a stranger than to say it to someone who has been close to us for a long time. We hope that the stranger would understand us well, that he perhaps wouldn't judge us. And who could understand the cab driver better than me? I had spent the first half-decade of my life chasing after people and feeling unwanted and unloved all the while.

I didn't know what to say at the time. So I chose to remain silent.

After a few minutes, he continued, 'Sir, have you ever been to an orphanage?'

'No.'

'I can understand. You must not get much time out of your busy schedule to go anywhere. In fact, looking at you, it appears that you going on vacation after a long time. Am I right?'

'Right.'

'Sir, if you get some time, please visit an orphanage. When you look at the children there, your heart will be filled with an overwhelming sense of peace. You will wonder how life gives us everything and will understand the art of appreciation better than before. Whenever I sit alone, I always think about this. What was my mistake that my parents left me alone in this cruel world? Why did they not take me along with them? But the painful thing is that you never get any answer and you just try to fit into society.'

I just listened to him. And I knew somewhere he was feeling good to speak his heart out. It made me feel the same when I vented to my close friends.

'Sir, can I make a request?'

'Yes. Sure.'

'If you are not too busy tomorrow, please come to my

orphanage. We will all celebrate with cake, chocolate, and sweets. It makes the children happy and never lets them feel that they are alone in this world. Tomorrow the gates are open for all.' He gave me a card with the address.

'Sure, I look forward to visiting it.'

Soon I saw some residential areas, with buildings rising up and a market circling around. I understood that we had entered Shimla.

We reached Shimla much before dusk. I had booked a room in a guesthouse. I didn't have much difficulty in locating it and the cab driver, as it is, knew the path very well. He left me in front of the guesthouse.

It was an exotic-looking building—a palatial wooden castle with state-of-the-art amenities. I checked in and got my room key.

The bellboy picked up my luggage and helped me to my room.

It was perfectly clean and looked great. The first thing I checked out was the bathroom. The basin and everything were very clean. It had become chilly in the room, so I switched on the heater. I kept my bag on the table and walked around, opening the window. My eyes went wide looking at the gorgeous view. The snow-capped mountains dazzled in the last rays of the sun. The calmness and breathtaking beauty gave me new life. I stared at such panorama till I heard a knock. Housekeeping had brought me a fresh towel and the room-service boy came in with the bowl of hot soup that I had ordered at the reception itself.

He asked me in a very polite tone, 'Sir, are you planning to go anywhere?'

'I haven't given any thought to it so far. Probably yes. Why?' I asked.

'Sir, there is a chance of heavy snowfall after dusk. Around 8 pm. So all our guests have been advised not to go too far. Let us know if you need any kind of help.'

'Sure,' I replied briefly. And he left the room.

I refreshed myself and changed into a fresh pair of jeans and a shirt. It was cold by this time. So I also put on a cardigan.

I checked the time. It was still 6.30 pm. I entered the balcony with my soup. Within ten minutes, it started snowing lightly. I rushed inside the room to get out my camera and capture the first snow of my life.

Feeling energetic after such a refreshing welcome to Shimla, I thought I would go out exploring. I bundled up in a coat and gloves and left the guesthouse.

The wide, airy streets were marvellous. I started clicking pictures of whatever I found beautiful, be it leaves, trees, streets, or wooden houses. I strolled from one street to the next. I found myself wandering past delightful rows of old timber-front houses.

Keeping the words of the hotel boy in my mind, I didn't go too far and returned in an hour.

I came back to my room after having dinner in the

guesthouse's restaurant. In the quiet, I observed some newness in me. It was probably due to the wonderful view and the deep valley in which I was able to submerge my worries, and the cool breeze swept the sadness off my face.

Next morning, I was fully prepared. I had slept peacefully the previous night, only to wake up when daylight peeked through the edges of the curtains.

I woke up fully, walked to the window, and parted the curtains. The light outside was still not bright but the air was very fresh. I could see the mist across the mountains and the snow-covered trees. The streets were still vacant and there was hardly anyone around. In this quiet hour, I planned for the day. I checked the wedding invitation that I had thrown onto the table. And pondered over where to go.

My phone rang. It was Mom. 'Hello.'

'Hello, good morning, beta. How is Shimla?'

'It's perfect. Thanks for pushing me to go there. It is absolutely stunning.'

'Great. Do you remember something?'

'Yes, I do. I know I have to attend the wedding and bring chocolate for you.'

'Yes.'

'In fact, I was checking the address of the venue at this very moment.'

'Nice. Yes. Enjoy yourself and attend the wedding.'

'Yes. Definitely.'

I had breakfast and around ten, left the guesthouse for

sightseeing. After I had visited all the nearby places, it was evening and time to set out for the wedding. I called for a cab and gave the driver the wedding card.

He knew the address. While on the way to the banquet hall, I asked him about the orphanage address. He thought for a moment, probably trying to recall it, and then said, 'Sir, there will be a U-turn from the place you are going to the right. The orphanage is in the opposite direction.'

'Okay,' I said.

'How long will it will take to reach the banquet hall?' I asked.

'Hardly twenty minutes if the road isn't blocked with snow. Last night, there was heavy snowfall. So most of the roads are jammed. Let's hope that the authorities have removed the snow.'

'Okay.'

I grew impatient. I didn't know what to do. The words of the first cab driver were still lingering in my mind. I was lost in thought.

Why was I going to attend the wedding? I wasn't at all interested. I knew my parents' friends would ask me the same set of questions. And I didn't want to answer them. It irked me. Though I had assured Mom I would attend the wedding, this trip was meant to free myself from my preoccupations and the memories that had wasted several years of mine. What did I get? Nothing. This trip was another way to get out of everything, to explore new places. Not to attend this boring wedding. If I attended the wedding like everyone else, it would perhaps be foolish. I had another place to go that I had never been. The words of the cab driver, the feelings of the children in the orphanage haunted me. I must go and meet those lovely children, must go to have a good time with them, to make them smile. No one was there to care for them. I would regret it if I didn't go there.

I decided not to go to the wedding. I asked the driver to turn back and drive me to the second address.

12

A FEW WEEKS LATER.

'Mom, I am going to the library,' I yelled, putting on my shoes.

'Library? You went there just two days back. How many books are you going to read? Why don't you go out and meet your friends? It has been several months since you have visited them. I forgot to tell you that Rakesh had come over to meet you while you were in Shimla.'

'Okay. What he was saying?'

'Nothing much. Just said that you hadn't spoken with him in quite a long time. And that you both haven't met in a while.'

'Oh, I will meet him next weekend. As of now, I am going to library to return these book returned and issue some new ones. It has been months since I have read anything new,' I said, showing her the books.

'Okay. Good. Very good. Remain in your room all the

time, deep into books. There's no life in books. Just live like an oldie. I won't say anything. When did you ever listen to me?'

'Mom, not again.' And ignoring her emotional blackmail, I left the house.

It was twilight. The library wasn't too far off but I would still take my car. However, today I avoided it deliberately. The weather was lovely and a cool breeze was blowing as it had rained that day. I enjoyed the stroll to the library.

It was almost empty. Perhaps people had avoided it because of the rain and now might be out for some refreshment in this weather. I submitted my old books and moved towards the fiction section.

Though I am a practical man, sometimes remaining in the fictional world brings me solace. It felt good that everything happened in books in a planned manner and at a slow pace. The lives in books were definitely utopic but to read about them brought me some sort of peace. I hardly touched romantic books in the fear that I would remain partnerless unlike in the book. Even in such an unreal world, the hero always found someone for himself, so I deliberately avoided such books.

'Huh. Not a single good book in the library,' I said to myself. As it had been quite a long time since my last visit, I was expecting something good. I moved towards the other racks.

This was when I saw Shagun. I had first seen her at the orphanage in Shimla and had instantly known that it wasn't going to be a one-time affair. Something inside me urged me to believe that she was perhaps the one I was looking for, that she was my soulmate, as Gaurav would say. But I couldn't muster up the courage to approach her. My shyness or my past heartbreak equally dried up my spirits.

I quietly returned to my room.

Office kept me busy. Client meetings, presentations, conferences consumed my entire mind and when I returned to my room, I was completely drained.

Thoughts of Shagun didn't come to me even once in the daytime, but at night, when I lay in my bed, my mind was uneasy. Even in this state of tiredness, sleep seemed an alien to me. My mind started playing tricks on me, and all of a sudden her face flashed in front of my eyes, first as a blurry image slowly taking shape and, after a minute, clear as water.

It almost jolted me out of bed, and I ran out onto the balcony, cursing myself for not approaching her. I looked into the darkness. A night lamp illuminated the street. A beggar took his shelter under it. There was no one to be seen. The night seemed much darker to me now.

I came inside the room and looked at my watch. 2 am. There was still time to morning.

I pushed myself onto the bed again. Now I decided that tomorrow might be the day. At that moment, a feeling of peace and contentment took over me. I slept as if I hadn't slept for ages.

I woke up at 7 am. It was the most peaceful slumber I had ever had. The morning looked brighter. Perhaps because it was a new morning for me.

I ran to the library again with a new sense of joy. I didn't know whether I would find her there. But I was happy. As I entered, I saw her at once in the same place as the day before.

I was agape and for the very first time, happy at my luck. Wow, she is here, I said to myself. I kept staring at her face. I didn't know what to say. In fact, I wasn't able to believe my eyes.

I slowly went towards her. A new courage began to wake up inside me. My past failures, my shyness, everything seemed to have been knocked out from me at once.

I sat at the table next to her. She pushed her book a bit, tilted her eyes, and looked at me suspiciously. Then she resumed reading.

I bent forward and adjusted my chair and then, in an attempt to ensure a conversation, coughed. She again looked at me in the same way, and resumed reading.

'Which book are you reading?' I finally asked.

She put the book on the table at once, looked at me suspiciously again, then as if she had known me for years.

'This one. It's *Midnight's Children* by …' she said and I interrupted her.

'Yes, by Salman Rushdie.'

'Oh. You know it. Have you read this book?'

'Umm. Thrice …'

'Thrice! I mean, you liked it so much?'

'Yes,' I said.

She said melodramatically, 'Appearances might be deceptive but I feel that I have seen you before.'

'Where?' I was surprised.

'At the orphanage. Aren't you the guy who donated a lot of money last month? You must be a man of good fortune and heart.' She smiled.

'Why were you there?' I was intrigued.

'I like to go there once in a while,' she said.

'It's a library. I think we can't talk here. We should go outside.' I pointed towards the board which mentioned silence.

'I stay nearby. Not very far from the library. Do come over someday,' she said, and began to get up.

I too got up, and we moved towards the exit.

It was evening when I knocked at her door. For the last few hours it had been raining incessantly. It seemed as if the sky would start pelting stones in a few hours, if at all the rain continued. It drummed on the roof of my car and the car groaned. Water gushed into its pipes. When the driver started it, it jerked two to three times, picked up speed, and jumped, and suddenly stopped by itself. I asked the driver to get out and have a look. He looked at me with a hostile expression before climbing out and slamming the door, as if I were treating him like a slave. This morning in office I was contemplating on meeting Shagun. It was days since I had seen her, after the episode with the Salman Rushdie book in her hands. I should have talked more with her. I should have told her about the plot and how India's political history excites me! I kept looking out of the window with the rain beating against it. For some time I was afraid of it not stopping and of missing my chance at meeting her today. My colleagues, who were observing me acutely, mocked me, knowing the truth.

'Is there anything coming through the rain? A pigeon or something carrying a letter for you through this window?' one of them asked.

I laughed at his remark. 'Pigeons nowadays don't carry letters,' I said, and continued, 'No. I am waiting for this rain to stop. I have to go somewhere.' It was my good luck that it stopped raining after some time. I hurriedly left the office.

But my luck didn't stand. The rain picked up again halfway and the car was giving up. Her house was just a kilometre away. I could surely walk but by the time I'd reach I would be sloshed. I told the driver to wait till the rain stopped and then to find a mechanic nearby. It started raining harder as I sat there waiting. After a few minutes, I decided to sprint. I had a plastic bag into which I wrapped my mobile phone and ran towards her place. After I had rung the bell twice, she opened the door.

She looked fresh, untouched by the beating water. Panting and holding my breath, I said, 'Hi.' Shagun seemed a bit surprised to see me completely drenched and dripping. She replied, 'Hi. What happened? Why are you drenched?'

'Ah, don't ask. It's nothing but my bad luck. My broke down and it's been raining so heavily. So I ran.'

'But you could have taken shelter somewhere for a while, maybe under a tree or at bus stop. What's the point of this? You could get cold or fever.'

'Oh yes. Sorry. I forgot about that. But how could I be late? I told you that I would meet you at 6.30 and I am here,' I made a cute excuse.

She smiled at me. 'So punctual.'

'Yes. I forgot to tell you, "Punctual" is my middle name.' She laughed at me.

'If you allow me, can I come inside and then you can scold me. Your neighbours are looking at me. What would they think about you?'

'Okay, okay. Come inside. Get dry first. There's a blue towel in the bathroom here. Take that. I'll make you some coffee.' She hurried towards the kitchen.

'That's really nice of you. Thank you!' I exclaimed.

I went into the bathroom, picked up the towel, and wiped my clothes with it. I then came into the drawing room, trying in vain to soak up the water in my hair and on my face with it. I saw Shagun coming in with a tray laden with two coffee cups and some biscuits.

I sat on the sofa and started flipping through the newspaper kept on the table.

The coffee was very refreshing. I gulped it down and felt some heat returning to my body. After about half an hour, I said, 'So, shall we leave now?'

'Yes. I am ready. Just give me a minute. I'll get my bag.'

Unlike other girls, and to my surprise, she actually took two minutes. And we both came out.

My car was already with the mechanic, so we thought would take an auto. But we had to walk for a while before we saw one.

I thought of striking a conversation but it was too quiet and neither of us made any attempt to break the silence. Which I was beginning not to like anymore. I kept on looking at her, thinking she would say something, but her head was bent low and her eyes were darting over the pebbles on the road. I decided to keep mum as nothing interesting came to my head. While I was tensely thinking of what to say, she asked me, 'So where are you taking me? I don't know much about this place. I shifted here just two months back.'

I opened my mouth to answer her but when she continued to speak, I stopped myself.

'I have always been scared of this place. Bangalore was pretty cool. But stepping outside after evening is risky in Delhi.'

'Yes, I understand. In fact, though I am a man I too am scared of this place at times. I prefer to return home after office. I do not generally like to loiter around outside if I don't have any work.'

She nodded and said, 'You didn't answer my question.'

'And that was?' I replied.

'Where are we going?'

'Oh. Sorry. That's a surprise. See, I'll tell you one thing. I hardly give surprises to anyone. It's tough for me to digest any surprise; in fact, if someone tells me that there is a surprise for me, I ask them to reveal it to me already. So don't force me otherwise I would have to tell you. All you need to know is, it's beautiful. Now you can keep guessing.'

'Yes, but I have to make sure of that. You might turn out to be a rapist. What would I do then?' she taunted me.

I said, 'True enough,' and laughed.

We got off the auto and she walked ahead of me in her green kurti, her back straight, a big vanity bag on her shoulder swaying like a pendulum, her high heels and her steps lifting just slightly to the right in a straight line.

It has always been tough for me to interact with people informally. For the past many months, I had hardly spoken with an woman except for maintaining a professional relationship with female associates in the company. I had even got to hear that I was considered a khadoos in office due to my reserved nature and curt responses. I didn't bother or mind whatever they assume of me. I didn't hold any grudge about that. I wasn't conservative or arrogant but I just didn't feel the spark with anyone anymore, and flirting with someone unnecessarily was not my habit. But when I saw Shagun at the orphanage I felt something knocking on the old wood of my heart. And now I knew her story. She had grown up there as a child and had never known her parents. She had no idea of where they were and how she had reached the orphanage in the first place. But the caretakers at the orphanage gave her all the love that she deserved and which she thought she would never have. The kind of humility I saw in her filled my heart. She mingled perfectly with the kids and took great pleasure in listening to their stories. Her laughter was unmistakably splendid. To the children, she was as kind and empathetic as a mother. That very moment, I decided that I would be at peace with such a person. Now that I had started talking with her, I slowly let her know that I sought a soulmate, an ideal companion, and that she fulfilled all my requirements, that we had similar interests in music and reading. She did not decline my interest in her. In fact, she too took an interest in me from the very first day.

'Don't worry. I am not that kind of a guy.'

'So, how many girls have you asked out on this kind of an outing?' she quipped.

'Umm. Let me count.'

'Count? That's probably a big achievement.'

She looked at me. I tried to count speaking aloud.

'One ... one ...' and for the next few seconds, I kept showing that I was thinking but I wasn't, really.. One ... that includes you.'

'Yes, I got the final number. It's one. I mean it's only you.' She smiled broadly.

'Okay, leave this. So what's your story?'

'You know it already. I have never known my parents and at the orphanage they told me that my mother died while giving birth to me and my father met with an accident a year later but then my uncle came to get me to live with his family in Agra ...'

'No, not this one. You've already told me this. Your story. What you feel. Your likes and dislikes.'

'I don't know. No one has asked me about all this earlier. So haven't given it any thought.'

'Ah, okay. No problem. I have asked you now. So tell me. We have enough time. Don't tell me you are one of those who keep up with the rat race. It's disheartening. Because I am one of those people. See how old I have become.' I tried to lighten the conversation.

'Oh. Then, I'm sorry to say that probably I too belong to this category. In fact, I have also grown old, if we compare ourselves to that young couple out there.'

She pointed towards a couple behind a tree.

'Well. But I reject your supposition that we have grown that old. Leave this. Tell me about yourself. Think of something you like. Something you do to make yourself happy.'

'I like reading. Reading is fun. It helps me connect with people across the world.'

'That's true. I also used to read a lot but due to office pressure, I left reading. It has been months since I have read something.'

'Yes, but you should take out some time for it.'

'Sure. What do you like to read?'

'I like fiction, mostly. Though I read some non-fiction as well. But I'm not that much into it.'

'Yes. I can see. *Midnight's Children*. Have you finished it?'

'Not yet. I issued it from the library just the day we met there. I started reading it last night. You said you'd read it, right?'

'Thrice ...' but she interrupted me. I like it when someone interrupts me. It shows that the person in front of me is interested in me and my passion.

'Oh wow! That's nice. You liked it so much that you read it thrice. I like the way the novel begins.'

'No, I tried to read it thrice but couldn't complete it. The language is so tedious and I couldn't connect with it. But I have always wanted to read Rushdie's novels.'

'Oh.' She felt embarrassed at my confession. 'So do you write also?'

'No. Not really.'

'Oh. By the way, shall we take an auto again?'

'How far is your surprise from here?' she asked.

'Not too far. Maximum twenty-minute walk,' I said.

'Then it's fine. We'll walk. I like walking. It's also stopped drizzling. Is it okay for you?'

'I am okay in every situation.' I took out some chocolate from my pocket and offered it to her.

After a moment's hesitation, she took it. 'You like chocolate?' she asked.

'Yes, very much. In fact, I carry chocolate with me at all times. Whenever I get irritated or sad, I eat chocolate. It makes me feel good.'

'That's nice. Then you can't be a rapist.' And we both laughed together.

Soon we reached the place. I excitedly said, 'Here it is, the famous Rooftop Café.

She looked surprised and her sparkling eyes revealed her emotion.

'You know the specialty of this place?' I asked.

'No. I haven't come here before,' she said.

'Its specialty is that you can view the beauty of the entire city while sipping on a drink and devouring delicacies. Let's go in.'

The doorman saluted and held open the door for us. We entered. I continued, 'The best thing about this restaurant is that you get to watch the whole serene environment from a high point. It's beautiful and romantic for hopeless lovers!'

I had already made a reservation for two. The manager showed us to the table. It was on the far side of the roof.

I pulled out the chair for her. I had learnt that such polite gestures always make girls happy.

She looked around and said, 'You are good with your choices.'

I called the waiter, 'Could you get me a choco frappe. And what would you like to drink?'

'Hot chocolate.'

Soon the waiter came up to the table with our drinks. I signalled to him to move away as I didn't want to lose the moment to serve Shagun her cup.

'Here you go, ma'am. Do you want to sit here or walk till the fence?'

'Let's walk.' As we walked towards the fence, she exclaimed, 'Wow! The view is majestic!'

'This is so amazing. Do you come here often?' she asked, taking a sip of her hot chocolate.

I smiled and said, 'Not really. I have come here twice. The first time, I came with my office colleagues. I liked the restaurant so much that I thought of coming next time with someone special. But there was no one special enough to accompany me. So I came alone.'

She laughed. 'I wish I had something even close to it near my place. It's like the sky blends with the hills. Exquisite!'

I didn't want to turn the moment into another evening

narrating our story, so suddenly I changed the topic and said, 'I know. Hey, look at the crescent moon. Isn't it beautiful? The moon has never failed stir passion into my soul. I always wanted to be an astronaut.'

'Really? Then how did you land up in the sad, bad corporate finance world?'

'Because Kalpana Chawla died.'

'Then what happened?'

'Along with her went my dreams.' I tried to enact a sob, but I sounded awkward and ended up with a false gasp.

She chuckled at my unsuccessful attempt at acting. I sheepishly said, 'Okay, enough acting.'

Shagun, sipping her drink, seemed ignored my confession and said, 'Do you see that?'

'See what?'

'The pattern. I always trace out patterns in the sky. Look at that big one towards your left. Doesn't it look like someone's flying?'

'Well, that must be Superman! Look at the hand. It looks like he has made a fist. Yeah, he has become old and now wants support to land properly on the ground, hence he wants a walking stick!' I mocked

'Whoa, what an imagination! I suggest you start writing a book.' Shagun looked at me, her eyes twinkling with amusement.

We both laughed. Later, we had a delicious dinner

together. The way she laughed, I assumed she liked being with me.

I also liked Shagun. I liked her gestures, her mannerisms. I liked conversing with her. I liked the way she asked about the Superman thing. I liked that she was a professor at the Department of English at the university. I liked everything about her. I didn't want to mention to her again how much I had liked the first time I saw her. I didn't know anything except her name at that time.

But it seemed that according to what Gaurav had predicted, my stars would be soon be favourable. I counted the number of years on the tip of my fingers. It had been more than six years.

13

HE WAS CORRECT.

We were at the park. Running my fingers through her hair, I was looking at her. There were several things that were speeding past in my mind. It was true that Shagun completed me and was someone whom I waited so long. She was now with me and I was going to marry her in the coming months. I knew her but did she really know me? Once I had posed this question to Gaurav and he had said that I should spend as much time as I could with her. She would learn about me and I would learn about her. And in the meantime, she would get to know the real Sameer. Gaurav said that he knew I had changed a lot in the past few years, but that one cannot change one's basic nature. Once I would spend time with Shagun, as she would start accepting my little quirks, then everything would fall in place and I could just be myself, not burdened with impressing anyone. It wasn't as easy as he made it out to be. I wanted her to know my eccentricities because whatever anyone says—it might be candlelight that is required to impress someone—at the end it is understanding, care, and trust that keep a relationship going. What if my eccentricities irritated her later? What if she suddenly came to know that I get angry easily though I had never got angry in front of her so far? What if she came to know that sometimes I become rigid and refuse to unbend? Would she able to stay with me? Mom had also told me that when she was sometimes irritated with me, she wondered how my life partner would be ready to stay with me, that I was beyond anyone's understanding. That she couldn't understand me in these thirty years.

Knowing the real me would probably not be the best idea, I thought. It wasn't that I viewed myself as a mean or cruel or stubborn man but it was true that I didn't belong to the crowd and it took a lot of time to understand me. Though I had been able to control my anger in the last four to five years. Perhaps because I mostly maintained professional relationships with people and allowed hardly anyone to come close to me.

When I was silent for some time, Shagun interrupted my thoughts, 'What are you thinking? You didn't even have the ice cream. It's yummy!'

'I wanted to tell you something. Everyone finds it trivial but I feel it's important,' I said.

'What are you talking about? Tell me.'

'I'm just telling you right at the beginning that I have some flaws.'

She seemed amused but maintained a neutral expression. 'Really? I always thought you are Aamir Khan, Mr Perfect.'

'No, Shagun. Hear me out. I am serious. I just think you should know the real Sameer before we get married.'

'In case I change my mind?'

'I wouldn't wish that but I also don't want to keep you in the dark about my small but many eccentricities.'

'Like what?'

'I get irritated if I don't get a reply. Be it textual or verbal. I don't know why. I am patient with most people most of the time but I do not like to be devalued and taken for granted. If I do, I lose my patience. I am very understanding but I want the other person to be accurate about his or her needs, otherwise I feel that the person is just whiling away his or her time with me. I mean, I try to behave my best with people … I mean there are many …'

Trying to maintain a serious expression, she nodded, 'I think I can handle your eccentricities. As many as they might be. However, when it comes to replies, I do reply to you always. Isn't it?'

'Yes, you do. I am just talking about my flaws. And sometimes, I do bend myself in a way the other person wants from me but other times, when I need someone, that too urgently, I don't listen to anything. In fact, I care about every other person's activities and schedules and if

I ask someone to do to something and it is necessary and he doesn't do it, I get angry within seconds. Though I try my best to control it.'

'Sameer, you are unnecessarily thinking too much. At the end of the day we are human,' Shagun came close to me and I could feel her breath as she spoke to me. She rubbed my hands as she said, 'Tell me, is there any space for judgment in love? Would we really judge someone whom we love with all our heart? Acha, leave apart romantic love, have you ever judged your mother or father for having not understood you in certain situations and conditions? No, right? The same goes for your partner who would love you selflessly. It is not about accepting and taking pleasure in your goodness but in accepting you as a whole with all your attributes, however otherworldly they might seem.'

She seemed to be as wise as if she had lived a thousand years. And I was only a germinating seed. I felt small and silly at her maturity.

'You understand, Shagun, but the world doesn't,' I said, looking into her eyes.

'You don't need the world, do you?' she asked. 'And your heart has the answer though you may not be able to articulate it in words,' she reassured me.

'I want to. But looking at how my life has taken shape over the last many years, I am just too apprehensive at times. I am scared, Shagun. What if ...'

She interrupted me by pressing my hand. 'You must.

This moment will never come back, Sameer.'

'Shagun, I want to spend the rest of my life with you. I want to be with you—today, tomorrow, forever.' I fumbled a bit as I popped the final question. 'Will you marry me?"

She smiled gently. I felt a shiver run down my spine. What would she say? I kept staring at her.

'Look at you. You are nervous like a school kid in front of his teacher! Aren't you?' she laughed.

'Shagun, please say …' I was on the brink of begging. I couldn't wait to hear her answer.

She could see my helplessness in my eyes and the same time she was aware of my love for her. That now, it had no bounds and had broken all shores.

She came close and put her head on my shoulders as she said, 'Sameer, that never needed answering. I have been in love with you since the time you spoke with me in Shimla. My heart has been yours since then.'

I felt stunned and ecstatic at the same time. I can't say I was shocked. I was too emotional to even detect such a feeling. Everything inside me changed and unfurled. A silent tear dripped down my cheek and I wiped it secretly. Years of waiting and years of hope were giving way to a changed perspective and I found myself in the garden of delight once again. My life was now moving towards a new place and I felt complete.

Next day, at home, while Mom sat in her armchair busy knitting a sweater for Dad, I came close and put with my head on her lap.

'Wah, today my beta has time for me!' she smiled. 'There must be something you wish to tell me. Chal, stop buttering me, tell me what it is? Is it a girl? Oh please, for god's sake tell me it's a girl.'

I smiled and she could make out that I was blushing. She had never seen me in such a state. She looked elated and didn't let me be at peace when I told her about Shagun. However, I felt an itch to tell her about Shagun's past. That she was an orphan and how she had lost her parents. That she had grown up in an orphanage and never received her parents' love. I didn't know how Mom would take it. But I had to try. So after having told her everything, I finally came to it, 'Mom, there is something that you may find a bit awkward. But I must tell you.'

'Why? Is she handicapped or divorced? Hey bhagwan, tell me!' Mom flushed.

'No, no. Nothing of that sort,' I pacified her. 'She is perfectly fine. And she's just the kind of girl I want, as I have told you. The only thing about her is that she doesn't have parents. She hasn't even seen them and doesn't remember them. Her mother passed away because of a birth injury and her father dies in an accident. She lived in the orphanage I had visited in Shimla until her uncle's family took her in.'

She looked stunned for a while and then gloomy. She didn't say anything. I knew this would happen. My mother had certain conventional notions about how her bahu should be. But I believed she wasn't bad at heart.

'But beta, what about people? I can still accept her. I know you have waited for the right person for so long. And at this juncture of life I would accept anyone as my bahu. I am just a bit weary of people. I mean, our relatives and the people we have known.' She sighed.

'Mom, people are not going to live my life or, for that matter, help me in any emotional or physical crisis. They only know to talk. And believe me, whoever I may marry, people will try to find flaws in her. It is in their nature. You cannot really give in to their gossip and mindless advice,' I tried to explain to her.

She held my hands and looked into my eyes. I could see her face softening.

'Beta, I just want you to be happy. Bring her tomorrow. She will be my daughter now onwards.'

We smiled and for the first time I felt that life was worth living for. And that a mother always understood her child even when everything failed.

I brought Shagun home the next day to introduce her to my mother. She took great pleasure in getting to know Shagun. In fact, I could see them getting along very well at the first meeting itself. Mom showed her the kitchen and told her that from now she would handle everything. Shagun was almost in tears and hugged Mom. I felt that everything was finally taking shape and was in its right place.

Over the next few days, my mind wandered and stalled at the same time. Everywhere I went, I contemplated on how I had spent my life and I had changed as a person. How love and its perilous search had torn me and the same time brought me together. It was difficult to hold myself for so long. But then, Mom and Dad always seemed to provide the comfort and solace of hope though they couldn't fully understand what I went through inside my head. The past haunted me and I could never successfully put a veil on it, lock it, and throw it into the river of despair. All of this, of course, until Shagun came along. And then everything unfolded like history on a paper and changed its course.

Just a week before our wedding, when our cards had been distributed, I called up Gaurav. It had been a few years since I had seen him.

'Hey man! Congratulations. Didn't I tell you it would take six years?' he exclaimed over the phone.

'Yes, yes! It truly did. Thanks to you,' I remarked sarcastically.

'Thanks to your fortune, buddy! And thanks to that beautiful girl who found her light in you,' he said, comforting me.

I felt good that people around me were so happy about my life. They were my friends in their truest sense of the word.

'Gaurav, thanks man! Honestly. You've helped a lot.'

'Ah, come on!' he said dismissively. 'Acha, I'm coming

down tomorrow, do send your chauffeur to pick me up. I'll be a bit early as I have to meet a couple of tarot clients that I have fixed up in your city. I plan to stay at your place until the wedding,' he said authoritatively. He, of course, had that kind of a right on me. All my close friends did.

'Yes, yes! Of course, buddy. You just come. My wedding would just be incomplete without you.'

My wedding was the following week. Everything, as they say, was perfect. Shagun was happy and I was elated beyond measure. What I had waited for so long was finally going to be mine. I had found love.

Shagun felt a sharp ache inside her. She realized that the power of love is just the same as the power of innocence. What she had thought were Sameer's nonsensical, desperate ideas at the beginning was actually his innocence. She was loved beyond measure and she was now convinced, irrespective of any doubts, that she could never find another person who would love her the way Sameer did. Tears flowed down her cheeks as she missed him. Nostalgia gripped her and she pined to be touched by him. The sliver of doubt that had pierced her was now healed and her undulating heart came to a standstill. She only had to wait for Sameer to return now. It felt like ages, yet the pleasure of waiting was irreplaceable with any other. There was pain and ecstasy at the same time. Not only had her love for Sameer grown, but also her respect for him. All the years that she had longed for her parents' love were fulfilled through Sameer. Keeping his diary close to her heart and thinking about his return, she slept off. The wind in the other part of the world grew cold and Sameer felt something piercing his soul. He felt the cold tugging at his heart. He longed to return and see Shagun, even if it was for a single day, a single night, a single minute.

EPILOGUE

I WAS NOW MINUTES AWAY from home. The flight had landed at an odd hour. I was unable to find a single cab at 1 am. There were no cabs even at the counter. I moved out with several passengers and broke into a brisk walk, pulling my bag behind me. It was tiring, but the thought of seeing Shagun gave me strength.

The previous week, when my new boss had come to know of the weird situation in which I had arrived in Switzerland, he called me into his office to have a word with me. He insisted that I go back to India and bring my wife to Switzerland. I had happily acquiesced and got my tickets done. My visa was still valid so I didn't have any trouble. I just had to see Shagun. Her radiant face brimming with laughter came to me in snatches during the entire journey. I wanted to be with her, hold her close, and tell her how much I had missed her. She must be missing me too, I was sure.

As I walked down the empty cobbled street, my steps echoing, I saw a line of autos. I asked a driver if he was willing to go till my place. He seemed to be a godsend, as he nodded and gestured for me to get inside with my luggage.

The moment I entered the house, Mom came running to me, 'Arre, why didn't you inform us that you were coming? Did something happen at work, beta? Chalo, it's good that you have come back.'

'Mom, I got some leave so I decided to come home.' I smiled at her.

'Ah, uff! Anyway, come in, come in. At least you have come. Do you know how much I have missed you?' She came close to me and kissed my forehead. Dad stood by my side, patting my back. He seemed to be proud of me. I embraced him and looked around for Shagun.

'Mom, where's Shagun?' I asked.

'Oh, she must be asleep. She came back late from the university and had to check a lot of assignments. I gave her some haldi-wala milk. She went to sleep just an hour back.'

I went inside the room and found Shagun's face pressed against the pillow. Her hair was scattered and tangled on the white sheet. She looked like an abandoned little girl. There were no lines on her face and her eyes, though closed, looked as if they were meant to sleep peacefully. Such peace on the face of a person was only possible if one had peace at heart. A brown diary lay at the side of her pillow. It looked familiar. My heart skipped a beat when I realized what it was. She had found my diary. My beautiful world was rocked on a cliff and I felt it would crumble any moment. Just when I was about to grab hold of the diary, she put out a hand towards it. She had her eyes open now and looked at me. I could see nothing but delight on her face. But I was perhaps too ashamed by then, that she had come to know all of me. I immediately jumped into self-explanatory justifications.

'Shagun, the diary not true. I am no longer the person I was, Shagun, believe me.'

She was still lying on the bed, her hand holding mine. She kept looking at me and smiling but didn't answer. She pulled me down and had me sit close to her.

'Shagun, I really don't know what to say. I have loved you with all my heart and I honestly have no proof of that, except my words. I don't know ...' I lowered my head and covered my face with my hands, not knowing what more to say.

She sat up and pulled my hands away from my face, and hugged me. For a few seconds, she ruffled my hair with her fingers and in a single whisper said what I had longed to hear since I knew of love.

'Sameer, come what may and whatever you may be today, I have and I will always love you, just the way you are.'

ACKNOWLEDGEMNETS

TIME REALLY FLIES AND here I am with my third novel—the story that I always wanted to tell, that was inside me for a very long time, is finally here. I feel immensely happy thinking that how in these years things have changed for me—my life and everything around me. I thought I would be able to tell only one story but with time, as I started meeting people, new stories kept forming in my head. This novel is also a result of the same. But it didn't happen overnight. In fact, it took a lot of pain because after writing half the script, I lost my laptop and didn't have the draft copy saved anywhere else. That time was very frustrating but I recalled a quote by Thomas Edison: 'There is a great value in disaster because you can start all over again.' This quote motivated me and, having no other option, I started all over again, trying to recall what I had written earlier, but couldn't capture much. At last, after working day and night, the book turned out to be the way I had visualized in my mind. I believe writing a new book is a new journey but something that can't be done alone. There are several great people who accompanied me during this journey and made it smooth during the frustrating times.

I thank my mom and dad who supported me throughout this journey, encouraged me, and gave me the freedom to do what I wanted to do. My brother and sister, thanks to you both for being part of this journey.

Gaurav Deka, thanks a lot. This book happened because of you. It was tough to write this one without your help and support. And I really feel sorry for pestering you during your Europe tour. Thanks for helping in every possible way and listening to my questions, without showing your frustration and understanding the situation. Rakesh, thank you. It's rare to find friends like you. Special thanks to both of you for reading drafts of the manuscript over and over again, helping to me finalize the script, remaining with me when things looked dark, and offering every possible help.

I want to express my gratitude to all my lovely readers who bought my book, read it, and took pains to connect with me on social media or through email. I thank you from the bottom of my heart. It is your love and affection that were pillars of support to me during dark times.

Surabhi Priyadarshini, thank you for listening to unnecessary details of the book, laughing at my poor jokes, and empowering me through my rough days despite your tight schedule.

Gurveen Chadha, thanks for giving me the opportunity to come up with this story. Pallavi Narayan, thank you for your careful, wise, razor-sharp editing and for sorting out my unnecessary queries, offering me the best possible solutions, and making the process smooth for me. Thanks to the entire Random House team for helping me at every stage of publishing.

Lastly, my deepest and sincere thanks to all of you who remain connected with me and have faith in me.

A NOTE ON THE AUTHOR

Sanjeev Ranjan is an ardent lover of western classical and instrumental music. He enjoys reading and has a keen interest in understanding human behaviour and relationships. He is currently pursuing his MBA from the Indian Institute of Foreign Trade (IIFT), Kolkata. He is the author of *It's No Longer a Dream* (2014) and *In Course of True Love!* (2012). This is his third novel.

Follow him at www.facebook.com/sanjeev.ranjan91 and www.twitter.com/sanjeevranj or email him at sanjeevranj91@gmail.com.